JESSICA WATKINS PRESENTS

CREED 2

Black Widow

by PHOENIX DANIELS

I'd like to give a very special thank you to L.A. Witt, the "wokest" Caucasian that I have ever had the pleasure of reading. This talented author posted a Facebook rant that turned into Governor Creed's press conference speech. I encourage my readers to run to www.gallagherwitt.com and check out this very talented author.

WHERE WE LEFT OFF...

"Dinner was amazing, sweetheart," Taylor complimented. "I love it when you cook."

"Oh yeah? You think your family liked my cooking?" Victor asked, peeking out of the kitchen.

"They loved it, babe."

Taylor walked around her living room, picking up empty beer bottles and tossing them into a trash bag. They were cleaning up after her and Victor's informal engagement party.

When she purchased her house, she never would have believed that the very first event that she'd be hosting in her home would be her engagement party. Their *official* engagement party would be held at the governor's mansion where they'd met. Taylor would be lying if she were to say that she was looking forward to celebrating her engagement with a bunch of strangers. However, she *was* marrying the governor, so she would have to acclimate herself to his lifestyle.

"Taylor, we really could've hired a cleaning service to do this!" Victor shouted from the kitchen.

"Um-mm, I don't like people touching my stuff."

Victor entered the living room, tossing a dish towel over his shoulder. "That's funny because you never seem to mind when *I* touch your *stuff*," he teased.

"That's cuz you know how to handle my *stuff*."

Victor chuckled and hugged her from behind. "It's wonderful how well our families got along," he remarked.

"Yeah. And, oh my God, did you see the sexual tension going on with Luc and Bella?"

"Not to mention Linc and Kenyatta," Victor grumbled.

"Lord, have mercy," Taylor sighed. "Oh, and our mothers… together, they're gonna be trouble. They were practically planning our wedding without us. And your dad…" Taylor giggled. "He thinks that because of me, you've got the black vote on lock."

"Yeah, but he might be right about that. The old man knows his politics," Victor muttered.

"You wish." Taylor laughed. "Shit, I'm a cop. You might lose a few black votes."

"As long as I have you, sweetness, it doesn't matter."

"Aww, ba-byyyy," Taylor purred.

Taylor sighed and closed her eyes, relaxing against his solid body.

"Gimme this bag. Come here," Victor said, taking the garbage bag and leading Taylor to the sofa. "Sit. You've been running around all day, making sure that this party turned out okay. You must be exhausted."

"Naw, baby, I'm good," Taylor assured.

"Sit."

Taylor sat and looked up at him with wide eyes. "Should I bark and roll over next?"

"Later," he quipped, tossing a bottle into the bag.

Taylor chuckled. Victor was right. She had had a busy day. Hell, she'd had a busy year. It had been two months since Victor asked her to marry him. She was just barely coming to terms with everything that had happened the months before, and now she was about to jump right into wedding-planning mode. It wasn't that she was unhappy about her engagement, she just wished that they could have a small ceremony or maybe a destination wedding. She could use a little quiet.

Taylor quietly watched as Victor cleaned. She leaned back against the pillows and thought of all the things that she and Victor had never discussed; one of those things being her job. Victor had never hidden his desire for Taylor to take an inside job if not quit altogether. She had no intention of quitting, but she did realize that security issues and the press were going to be a hurdle. Since Victor put the beautiful diamond on her finger, it seemed as if they purposely avoided such conversations.

"Taylor, are you okay?" Victor asked, snapping her out of thoughts.

His voice was filled with concern as he sat next to her.

"Um, yeah…Yes, I'm okay."

"What's on your mind? Talk to me."

Taylor sighed and leaned against him. Victor wrapped an arm around her and massaged her shoulder.

"Victor, it's been a crazy year; the shooting, the media, Maria getting shot, me getting shot, Gore, Candace, you shooting Candace. It's a lot to process. Now, we're getting married."

"Is it too soon?" Victor asked with a sad look in his eyes.

"No. No, baby. It's not too soon, but… okay…Where are we gonna live? And what about my job?"

"Well, where do want to live?'

"Shit, I just bought this house."

"Okay, then we'll live here."

Taylor narrowed her eyes and asked, "Really?"

"Yeah. I like your house. We'll have to make some security provisions, but I'm comfortable here."

"Oh, Victor, you are so fucking awesome," Taylor cooed, climbing into his lap.

"You say that now. But when the subject of the police department comes up, I'm sure you'll change your mind."

"Okay, then we won't talk about that today." Taylor chuckled.

"Good idea. Listen, with all the hell that you've been through, I just wanna give you some of the peace and security that Candace took from you. That part of your life is over. Now, well concentrate on our future. Candace couldn't take that away."

"See? That's the thing, babe."

"What's the thing?"

"The whole time we were in Candace's house, she never once copped to shooting me. She was shoutin' from the rooftop about how she shot Maria, but she didn't mention me or Collier at all."

"Hmm…" Victor contemplated. "You sure?"

"I'm positive. So, that leaves the question: how was Candace connected to Collier?"

"She wasn't."

Taylor jumped from Victor's lap at the sound of a female voice coming from her hallway. The beautiful, blonde intruder was standing between Taylor and the weapon that was in her bedroom, so Taylor prayed that the woman wasn't armed with the intention of killing them both.

"What the fuck are you doing in my house?" Taylor hissed.

"I came to congratulate you on your engagement to my husband," she said in a sugary but icy tone.

"What?!" Taylor gasped.

She turned to Victor just as he was slowly rising from the sofa. His normally tanned face had turned as white as a sheet, and he seemed to have stopped breathing. Taylor grabbed his arm when he stumbled slightly forward.

"Victor?" Taylor whispered to him, before shouting, "Who are you?!" at the blonde.

"S-she…she's," Victor stuttered. "Her name is Rosemary…Rosemary Creed. She's my wife."

CREED 2

by *Phoenix Daniels*

CHAPTER ONE

TAYLOR

Wife?

"Wait! You're *what*?" Taylor was sure that she hadn't heard Victor right, but when she looked up at him, she noticed that the color had completely drained from his handsome face. His expression was that of dazed confusion. "Victor?" Taylor called, in an attempt to wake him from the trance that the beautiful blonde had placed him in.

"Rosemary," he breathed, completely ignoring Taylor.

Taylor cringed at the way he'd said her name. And she certainly couldn't hide the feeling of sadness and abandonment when Victor left her side and hurried across the living room. When he pulled her into his arms, Taylor felt what could've been the equivalent to the sharp, hot pain of being shot in the chest. She folded her arms, in need of a hug, even if she had to do it herself.

Victor stepped back and took Rosemary's face in his hands. He was studying her as if he were trying to make sure that she was real. His hands on Rosemary's face made Taylor feel faint. She shivered, feeling instantly cold. Tears swam in her eyes at the very thought of losing Victor.

Even though Victor had told Taylor that he was never in love with Rosemary, he had admitted that he'd had great affection for her. He'd often said that, together, they'd made a great team. Their relationship was supposedly more of an alliance than a marriage. As she looked at the two of them, and the way they interacted, she was consumed with jealousy. But when Rosemary's hand rose to Victor's chiseled jaw, jealousy turned to *rage*.

"Victor!" Taylor gritted angrily.

Victor turned toward Taylor quick enough to avoid Rosemary's caress. Taylor crossed her arms and narrowed her eyes at him. Although his wife's return from the dead may have been a miracle in Victor's eyes, to Taylor, she was simply a woman in the arms of her man. Victor walked over to Taylor and placed a hand on her arm.

"Taylor, babe, it's just that…well, we all thought—"

"I know what you all thought," Taylor snapped. "You were all obviously wrong."

Taylor looked over at Rosemary. Victor's *dead* wife was a pretty woman. Closer to Victor's age, she possessed a graceful elegance that said she was from Victor's world. She was slim but curvy. She had thick, lustrous hair, and sparkling blue eyes. She was dressed impeccably. Her slacks were white, and her blouse was powder blue. She couldn't have been more contrary to Taylor, and her more relaxed style. Taylor glared over at Rosemary.

"What do you know about the shooting?" Taylor asked, staying on point.

Rosemary smiled at Victor. "Your wife to be is quite extraordinary, beautiful, and filled with fire. You chose well, Victor."

"Indeed," Victor agreed, placing his hand on the small of Taylor's back.

Taylor was not moved by Rosemary's flattery. She hadn't answered the question. "How are you not dead? And what do you know about me getting shot?"

Without answering, Rosemary walked over to Taylor's sofa and sat. "Do you have wine?" she asked in a bored tone. "I could use a drink."

"Are you fucking serious? Don't play with me, bi—"

"Taylor," Victor interjected. "Yes, we have wine. Let's calm down and have a rational conversation."

CREED 2
by *Phoenix Daniels*

Taylor couldn't believe her ears. She was looking at Victor as if he'd grown a third eye. Why was he so fucking calm? It was his *wife* who had ascended from the grave. "Victor, what is wrong with you? The woman just waltzed her ass in here as if she didn't have a funeral, and you seem totally okay with that. Why aren't you freaking out?"

Victor rubbed Taylor's shoulders while looking her in the eye.

"Because I want answers, my love. Don't you?"

Taylor blinked up at him. "Of course, I do, but—"

Victor smiled, exposing perfect, white teeth and adorable dimples. "I am surprised, Taylor, but I've seen entirely too much in my lifetime to let anything shock me into disbelief."

"Fuck that!" Taylor snapped. "She just 'Walking Deaded' her ass into my living room after…how many years? And now she wants to kick back and sip wine?"

"Taylor, baby, calm down. How can we get answers if you aren't willing to listen?"

Rosemary crossed one leg over the other and smiled at Victor. "I like her, Victor. She's feisty."

CREED 2
by *Phoenix Daniels*

Rosemary looked up at Victor, and in her eyes, Taylor saw what appeared to be sorrow, maybe even regret. She turned her attention to Taylor and patted the sofa next to her.

"Taylor, we need to talk. Please sit down so I can explain. I can prove to you that I am not the enemy. I only returned because I was afraid that you and Victor might be in danger."

Taylor sighed. She did need answers…answers that only Victor's wife could give. Forgoing the seat next to Rosemary on the sofa, Taylor sat in the chair, directly in front of her.

"How are you alive?" Taylor asked, getting right to the point.

Rosemary tensed. Her entire demeanor changed. She inhaled a deep breath. And, even though it was Taylor who had asked the question, her eyes were trained on Victor.

"As you probably know, in my past life, I was an immigration attorney. To make a very long story short, I stumbled upon a massive human trafficking ring with major conspirators. Some of those conspirators were very close to the top of the political food chain."

"How close?" Victor questioned.

CREED 2
by *Phoenix Daniels*

"As close as Senator Craven," Rosemary whispered as if someone other than the room's occupants would overhear.

"Henry?" Victor marveled with disbelief.

Apparently, Victor was capable of being shocked, but Taylor would put nothing past a politician. She would admit that she didn't expect the senator to be involved in something as inhumane as human trafficking.

Henry Craven, a senior United States Senator from Illinois, held the highest position in the Republican Party leadership in the Senate. Even though he was a Republican, the senator was favored by most citizens of Illinois, Republicans and Democrats alike. He was the current chairmen of the subcommittee on human rights and the chairman of the subcommittee of financial services in general government. Hell, even Taylor had voted for him.

"You can't be serious." Victor sighed.

"But I am," Rosemary confirmed, looking deeply into Victor's eyes.

Taylor watched Victor as he processed the information that Rosemary had just divulged. Because he had considered Senator Craven a friend, he was beyond disturbed. Although she felt for him, Taylor wanted Rosemary to get on with the rest of the story so that she could get the hell out of her house and go back to being dead.

"Go on," Taylor urged, with very little patience.

Rosemary cut her eyes Taylor's way, but when the dare sparked in Taylor's eyes, she was smart enough to stifle her comment. Instead, she continued.

"I discovered that the senator, among others, was working with human traffickers from certain countries to trick young women into migrating to the United States. They would help by providing whatever documentation that was needed to enter the country. The women were led to believe that there would be jobs waiting for them in the "land of the free." But when they arrived, they were stripped of their visas and sold into sexual slavery."

Taylor, unlike Victor, was not as stunned. Since she'd been on the police department, she'd seen plenty of heartbreaking cases involving human trafficking. "How?" Taylor asked.

"How, what?" Rosemary asked, confused.

"How did you discover this conspiracy?"

"Through one of my clients. She was lucky enough to escape. For a while, she found work as a domestic, but her immigration status was discovered. When she was arrested, she couldn't afford an attorney. My firm was on a pro bono rotation, so I was assigned the case."

Victor was still and quiet. Rosemary massaged her temple as if even thinking about the case was creating a headache. But Taylor was eager to hear the rest of the story.

"What does this have to do with your death?"

Rosemary inhaled a shaky breath before responding. "I went to a friend in the U.S. Attorney's office. She initiated an investigation that got her and my client killed."

Rosemary's cheeks flushed. Taylor could see sadness and regret etched across her pretty face.

"I'm sorry," Taylor whispered sincerely.

"Thank you," Rosemary mouthed.

"Wait," Victor injection. "Why didn't you go to your father? Phillip is one of the most powerful lobbyists in the United States. He certainly wields more power than Henry. Surely, he could have provided you with protection."

Rosemary sighed. Her baby blues eyes began to water. "I couldn't put my dad in danger. If something were to happen to him, I wouldn't be able to live with myself." Rosemary hiccupped and swiped a tear from her cheek.

CREED 2
by *Phoenix Daniels*

"My friend was brutally beaten and then shot four times. I just couldn't put anyone else in harm's way."

"Damn," Victor responded with a deep breath.

He walked over to Rosemary. She was so shaken that she was close to hyperventilating. Victor kneeled down in front of her, placed his hand on both shoulders, and pulled her into a hug. For some reason, that time, Taylor didn't mind as much.

Shit, she needed a hug.

Taylor sat quietly by as Victor comforted his…*wife*.

"Rosemary, your father is a powerful man. Surely, he can take care of himself. You should let him help you," Victor told her.

"You're wrong, Victor. This assassin had no problem killing a United States attorney and would have no problem getting to my dad. I had to run. If I hadn't, everyone that mattered to me would've been in danger."

Tears ran down Rosemary's cheeks. She sank into Victor's arms as she cried. Taylor was sympathetic to her pain. And before she could stop herself, she had crossed the room and kneeled next to Victor. She gently placed her hand on Rosemary's back. Rosemary, still sobbing, leaned over to place her head on Taylor's shoulder.

CREED 2
by *Phoenix Daniels*

"I'm sorry for everything that you've been through. It must have been horrible," Taylor softly consoled.

"Oh, Taylor, you have no idea. I had to not only survive a deadly hurricane, But I had to learn a new way of life. I had no money, no name, and no family. I did a lot to survive."

Victor looked up at Taylor and whispered, "I'll get wine."

"And tissue," Taylor said as he stood.

Once Victor was out of the room, Taylor asked, "How did you find out that it was the senator that put a hit out on you?"

"Collier," she admitted. "Collier had always been my eyes and ears. He kept me informed."

"Collier!" Taylor hissed, not at all surprised.

"There was a time when Collier loved me. I guess you could say that I had him wrapped around my little finger." Rosemary smiled sadly as she continued, "Well, he was until he started sleeping with Kara Edwards. Then, I guess he fell under her spell."

Taylor's jaw dropped when Rosemary mentioned Victor's former press secretary and jilted lover. "*Kara*

Edwards? What the hell does she have to do with this?" Taylor inquired, just as Victor reentered the room.

"Yes, Rosemary, what *does* Kara have to do with any of this?" he asked as he placed a bottle of Merlot and three wine glasses on the cocktail table.

Rosemary scrubbed her eyes with her fists and look up at Taylor with swollen, red eyes.

"It was Kara. She was the one who convinced Collier to shoot you."

CHAPTER TWO

BELLA

Bella jerked and sat up with urgency. She gasped from the rush of wind that hit her face when her supervisor, Sergeant Carver, dropped a manila folder on her desk.

"You're up, Devereaux."

Bella took a second to gather herself before pushing herself off of her desk. She was dazed and exhausted, trying desperately to focus on her sergeant. She'd been up most of the night combing through video from the hospital. She was looking for leads on Collier's killer.

Bella rolled her neck to stretch out the kinks and grabbed the file from her desk.

"Sarge, I'm already working a homicide," Bella grumbled as she opened the folder. "I'm still on the Sanders case."

"Nobody's gonna miss that dickhead. Put it aside and go hit the street. This case takes precedence. Besides, didn't your friend have him taken out?"

Bella rolled her eyes before she could stop herself. Most in the department believed that Taylor was responsible for Collier's death.

"There is no proof of that."

"Well, we got three dead girls and no available detectives. Go work the case."

Bella scanned the file as her sergeant disappeared into his office. Three dead women found near the University of Chicago was all of the preliminary info given. Bella assumed that they were more than likely coeds. She closed the folder and grabbed her leather jacket from the back of her chair. She checked the pocket for the keys to her department-issued, old-school Chevy Caprice, and left out of the very busy homicide division.

Twenty minutes later, Bella hit the scene and hopped out of her car. Uniformed officers were everywhere, no doubt, fucking up her crime scene. She walked past the officers, straight to the beat sergeant. His mood was dismal. Bella hadn't seen the bodies yet, but his demeanor indicated that she was walking into something grisly.

"Hey, Gary."

"Bella," he greeted in a deep rasp.

CREED 2
by *Phoenix Daniels*

"What you got for me?"

Gary sighed and turned toward the dilapidated old house. They were in a rundown, but up-and-coming neighborhood near the university. Bella's crime scene was the only house on the block that wasn't boarded up.

Bella carefully followed Gary up the porch stairs, praying that they wouldn't collapse. She frowned as she entered the front door, immediately pissed at the number of cops that were traipsing through her crime scene.

"Everybody out!" Bella shouted, causing the nosy cops to turn in her direction.

A few of the officers knew right away who Bella was and headed out the front door. But there were others who looked her up and down in assessment as if to say, 'Who the hell are you?'

Bella turned to the sergeant with narrow eyes. She couldn't believe that he'd allowed such shoddy police work.

"Don't look at me," Gary defended. "They were here when I got here." He turned to the few that remained. "You heard the detective. Out!"

Bella looked around the small house as the uniforms filed out. Luckily, there wasn't a lot of trash and debris. There was no furniture except for a few crates and a couple of pillows in the living room.

"Where are my bodies?" Bella asked the sergeant.

"Basement." Gary pointed to a door past the kitchen.

As Bella entered the kitchen, she scanned the floor for blood evidence. In the middle of the room, there was an old wooden table with three flimsy chairs. There was nothing on the table. In the sink, there were six empty beer bottles.

"Sarge!" she called out.

"Yeah," he responded from the threshold.

"Where's the E.T.?"

Bella wanted the evidence technician to collect the bottles. There was a possibility that they could extract DNA or fingerprints from them.

"I think he's in the basement."

He thinks, Bella scoffed in her head.

Gary hadn't done a damn thing to protect her crime scene. In Bella's opinion, professionalism began to diminish the moment the department created a test to determine whether officers should be promoted. Unfortunately, supervisors got promoted because they knew someone important, or they tested well, or they were handed the test in advanced. Sadly, because of that, some supervisors tended to have little common or street sense. Gary's lazy ass had to have fallen in one of those categories.

Bella rolled her eyes and walked over to the refrigerator. She pulled it open and looked inside. To her surprise, it was fully stocked, proving that the house wasn't truly abandoned. She closed the door and moved to the basement door. If she thought the house smelled like death before, death had been confirmed as soon as she opened the basement door.

Bella took a second to allow herself to adjust to the putrid aroma of rotting flesh before taking the first step down the dark stairway. She pulled out her flashlight from her back pocket and turned it on. When she made it to the landing, she noticed a light in a far corner. She heard movement as she made her way toward the light. Bella pointed her flashlight toward the walls of the dark, smelly basement. She was in search of a light switch. She figured since there was electricity in other parts of the house, there should've been electricity in the basement.

Bingo!

Bella found a light switch and flicked it on. She smiled when the main room of the basement was illuminated. As she inwardly celebrated, Bella made a mental note to find out who's name the electricity bill was in, *if* there was an electric bill. Nowadays, folks knew how to cipher electricity illegally.

"You startled me," a voice called out in the darkness. "I never thought to turn the lights on."

Bella strained her eyes to see the man in the dark corner. His uniform identified him as the evidence technician.

"This your case?" he asked.

"Apparently so. Detective Devereaux," Bella said, introducing herself.

"Bob...Bob Henry. Come. Your victims are over here."

Bob, the evidence tech, led Bella to the corner. The scent of death got stronger as Bella approached. She looked down at three, totally naked, dead white women. Her first question was, 'How did they wind up in this house, in this part of town?' The area that they were in wasn't exactly known for producing white bodies.

The women, who couldn't have been more than nineteen or twenty, appeared to have been badly beaten, and each of their throats had been slashed. It was a terrible bloody mess. Their hands were tied at the wrists and hoisted above their heads, and their ankles were also bound. The young victims were staring

up a Bella with dead, glassy eyes, and she could still see dried
tear stains on their cheeks.

Bella looked down to see if the evidence tech's shoes
were covered. They were. So, she took a second to grab shoe
covers from her bag before approaching the victims. Bella
slipped the covers over her own shoes and asked, "Where's the
ME?"

This was definitely a scene where the medical
examiner's presence was needed.

"En route," Bob responded.

The evidence tech handed Bella a pair of gloves. Even
though she'd brought her own, she took them.

"Come and look at this," he told her.

Bella put the gloves on and stepped closer to the
technician. He kneeled closer to one of the victims and lifted
her wrist. Bella squinted to see the small tattoo on her wrist. It
was a barcode with and a series of five numbers.

"They all have it," the tech revealed.

Bella tilted her head at the evidence tech.

"You a medical examiner?" she asked him.

"No, but—"

"Then stop touching my bodies," Bella ordered.

CREED 2
by *Phoenix Daniels*

"You tell 'em, girl," a feminine voice cosigned.

Bella smiled and turned toward Dr. NiYah Reed, Bella's childhood friend. She and Bella had been friends since the third grade. When they first met, they'd gotten into what turned into a schoolyard brawl over a game of hopscotch. Both, Bella and NiYah, had different versions of how the fight began and ended. And even though they were eight when it happened, their playground fight came up every single time they had a little Don Julio in their systems.

Bella chuckled as NiYah approached the victims. She slid on a pair of gloves and lifted the chin of one of the victims. When *she* touched the dead woman, Bella had absolutely nothing to say. After all, Dr. NiYah Reed was actually the medical examiner.

CHAPTER THREE

TAYLOR

It was three in the morning, and Taylor felt as if they had consoled Victor's wife long enough.

"So, where are you staying?" Taylor asked, ready to go to bed.

Rosemary blinked up at Victor with pleading eyes. "I don't have anywhere to go," she whispered.

"So, your plan was to come here and do what? Live with Victor? I'm sorry, honey, but that's not gonna happen."

Rosemary wiped the remaining moisture from her cheek and stood. She rolled her shoulders back and glared at Taylor. "I risked my life to come here and warn you about Collier. I had no way of knowing that he was dead until I got here," Rosemary blurted.

"No, you didn't. You could have called. Why did you *really* come back?" Taylor leaned back on the sofa and crossed one leg over the other. She returned Rosemary's glare as she waited for the truth.

"Victor," Rosemary confessed on a faint breath.

"It's a good question," Victor agreed. "What's the answer?"

Rosemary stood and began to pace nervously. She ran her fingers through her long blonde hair and turned to Taylor.

"Someone tried to kill me," she admitted. "Some woman put a gun to my head and forced me into the back of a limousine. She said that she'd been looking for me for a long time. No doubt, her plan was to kill me, but we had a car accident that killed the driver. I was dazed, but the woman was unconscious. So, I escaped."

Taylor noted just how different she and Rosemary were. If a woman had put a gun to Taylor's head and threatened to kill her, she would have made sure that said woman never regained consciousness.

Taylor reached for the bottle of Merlot and poured a moderate amount into all three glasses.

"Rosemary, I feel for you, but—"

"Taylor," Victor interrupted. "May I speak with you in the bedroom?"

Taylor narrowed her eyes at Victor and asked, "Why?"

"Now, please," was his abrupt response as he headed to Taylor's bedroom.

Taylor blew out a harsh breath and followed Victor into the bedroom.

"He hasn't changed a bit," Rosemary chortled at Taylor's back.

Taylor ignored the comment and walked into the bedroom, ready to do battle. But as soon as she entered, she was ambushed by Victor. He pulled her into his arms and grabbed the back of her head. He pushed his lips against hers and kissed her with a passion that rendered her immobile.

"I love you so much, babe," he professed when he ended the kiss.

It was amazing. With just one kiss, Victor had weakened her resolve. Her irritation had immediately melted away. There was a contentment that came with being in Victor's arms.

Taylor looked up, into her fiancé's beautiful eyes. "I love you too," she whispered.

Victor led Taylor to the bed and urged her to sit. Once she did, he sat next to her. Victor took her hand and smiled, exposing his beautiful dimples.

"Taylor, I know we haven't talked much about our past marriages, but I need to make you understand what Rosemary and I had."

Taylor knitted her brows as she waited for him to explain his relationship with Rosemary. But when he took too long to speak, Taylor asked, "Are you about to try to convince me that we need to take in your ex…um, your current wife?"

"Yes."

"What?" Taylor exclaimed. "You cannot be serious."

"Taylor, sweetheart, Rosemary is my friend. Yes, we were married, but I wasn't in love with her, nor was she in love with me. We got married for the optics. It was a purely political manipulation. Baby, what I'm trying to say is our marriage was never a real marriage."

Taylor nodded, and Victor smiled as if he were happy that he'd gotten through to her. He was about to stand when Taylor pulled him back to the bed by his shirt.

"Victor?"

"Yes, babe?"

"When you and Rosemary were committing your political manipulation, did you have sex?"

Victor's smile fell. He cleared his throat and rounded his shoulders. His expression and body language answered Taylor's question for him.

"That's what I thought. Get her out of here."

CREED 2
by *Phoenix Daniels*

Victor nodded his head. "Consider it done," he assured as he stood and left the bedroom.

✶✶✶✶✶

Taylor stood in front of the mirror and brushed her hair into a high bun. She was exhausted and grateful that she'd finally be able to go to bed. Victor had finally gotten rid of Rosemary. He'd ended up calling Gregor and instructing him to pick her up and take her to his penthouse in Storm Tower. Taylor wasn't too happy about Rosemary sleeping in Victor's place, but it was a compromise. She would only be staying one night. Lucas, Victor's younger brother, would be picking her up in the morning to take her someplace safe; hopefully someplace far away.

Taylor realized that she and Victor would eventually have to have a conversation about Rosemary's return and how it would affect their engagement. The woman had faked her death because she was running for her life, but exactly how was Victor supposed to divorce a dead woman? But the conversation would have to happen at a later time because when Victor stepped out of the bathroom, wrapped in a towel, Taylor's body reacted immediately.

She placed the novel she was reading on the nightstand and admired his masculine beauty. His thick, dark hair was still wet and slicked back, showing his perfectly chiseled features. Noticing Taylor's lustful perusal, Victor grinned, awarding her one sexy dimple.

"Damn, babe." Taylor sighed. "No man should be this fine."

Victor smirked. "Fine, huh?"

"Fine as hell," Taylor confirmed, lifting the sheets for him to join her in bed.

Victor removed the towel from his waist and used it to wipe the excess water from his muscular body. His flirtatious gaze never left Taylor as he stalked around the bed. His fresh, masculine scent, extreme beauty, and sex appeal caused a tightening in her core.

Victor slid into bed and reached for Taylor. He caressed her face and placed sensual kisses along her jawline.

"I love you," he muttered against her skin.

"I love you," Taylor purred.

CREED 2
by *Phoenix Daniels*

Victor flipped her on her back and climbed on top of
her. He pressed his wet, muscular chest against her breasts and
kissed her with a hunger that was the proof of his love.

CHAPTER FOUR

BELLA

Bella hopped out of her car and headed up the walkway. As soon as she ascended the steps, she took a breath and prepared herself to deal with her parents. Since she'd been working twelve-hour days, trying to solve two murder cases, Bella knew that she was going to get an earful about not spending time with her family.

Bella could smell the inviting aroma of her mother's cooking as soon as she hit the porch. Winona, Bella's mom, in her opinion was the best cook in the world. Her mom was Native American from the Chitimacha tribe in New Orleans. In the kitchen, she often combined her Native American heritage with her Cajun surroundings to create the most delectable dishes that Bella had ever had the pleasure of consuming.

Bella pulled the screen door open and knocked on the door. She checked the knob to see if the door was unlocked.

It was.

Bella twisted the knob and entered her parent's house. Her dad greeted her in the living room.

CREED 2
by *Phoenix Daniels*

"Belladonna Devereaux, where have you been, lil girl? We ain't seen you in weeks," her daddy reprimanded with open arms.

Bella rolled her eyes because her dad was greatly exaggerating. She ignored his fib and flew into his arms just like she always had as a little girl.

Since she'd chosen to be a detective in one of the most dangerous cities in America, Bella had dealt with enough to break the thickest branch on the strongest Oak. But her daddy's embrace always seemed to make everything in the big bad world seem better.

William 'Bill' Devereaux was Bella's hero. He was a black native of Shreveport, Louisiana. Bella's dad was a giant of a man. He stood at six-foot-five and he was bulky but not fat. He was well-respected and often feared. He was also known for his very low tolerance for bullshit. Bella's dad was a kind man. But when it came to his family, he was as protective as a pit bull.

"Bella, baby, have you heard from your sister?"

The sound of her mother's voice prompted Bella to peek around her dad's broad shoulders.

CREED 2
by *Phoenix Daniels*

"Hey, Ma. I'm fine. Thank you. How are you?" Bella sassed.

Bella stepped out of her dad's embrace and peered over at her mother. She was standing in the doorway, wearing her favorite apron. It read, 'Do not Disturb.'

Winona, Bella's mom, was tiny compared to her dad. He towered over her like a giant. Belladonna and her sister, Donatella, had inherited their mother's crimson complexion and long, straight, black hair. But in regards to their height, they were somewhere in between. They were nowhere near their dad's height but tall for girls.

"Hi, baby," her mother responded with a smile.

At fifty-five, Bella's mom hadn't lost one ounce of her Native American beauty. Winona had dark, sultry eyes, a proud sharp nose, and plump lips. Over the years, she'd maintained her fit, girlish figure.

Bella crossed the room and hugged her mom. She rubbed her mom's head and inhaled the familiar scent of love and security. Winona kissed her cheek and stepped back. She inspected Bella as she did every time she visited.

"I'm in one piece, Ma." Bella chuckled. "What'cha cooking?"

CREED 2
by *Phoenix Daniels*

"Hunter's stew and fried, green tomatoes," Winona responded with a grin.

Bella's smile widened. Her inner foodie was secretly dancing. Her mom was making her favorite. "Mmm-mm," Bella hummed, hugging herself.

Bella began to walk toward the kitchen, but her dad's booming voice halted her steps.

"You didn't answer your mother's question."

Bella squinted, trying hard to remember her mother's question, but the only thing that she could focus on was the aroma of the stew and a plate full of fried, green tomatoes.

"Your sister?" her mother reminded.

"Ohhh… No, I haven't talked to Donna in a couple of weeks," Bella admitted.

Winona folded her arms and frowned. "How on earth could you go weeks without talking to your sister," her mother fussed. "I thought that y'all were supposed to have some kinda special bond."

Bella's mother was referring to the fact that she and Donna were twins. She was right. They did share a bond. Like Bella, Donatella was a police detective. But unlike, Bella,

Donna worked undercover. There were times that the job required her sister to stay away for long periods of time.

Since, as a homicide detective, Bella was usually called after a violent crime has been committed, Donatella's job as an undercover officer was much more dangerous. However, she would never tell that to her parents. They worried enough about the two of them.

"Ma, Donna is fine. You know how she gets when she's on assignment."

"I'm sick of this," Winona fussed, shaking her head in frustration.

"Mama! Why are you mad at me? I'm actually here," Bella pointed out.

Bella's dad walked over, looked down at Bella, and placed a hand on her shoulder.

"Come on, pumpkin. Let's get some food in you."

Bella looked over at her mom. Winona smiled apologetically and nodded toward the kitchen.

"You coming?" Bella asked her mom.

"Honey, do you think I cooked all that food just for you?" Winona chuckled. "Go on. I'll be there in a minute."

CREED 2
by Phoenix Daniels

Bella was concerned about her mom when she went into the kitchen. She didn't have any children, but she could only imagine how fearful her parents must've been, having both of their daughters having such dangerous jobs. She understood why Donna was away so much, but her parents weren't cops, and they didn't. How could she and her sister expect them to understand? Her dad was a high school principal, and her mom was a dentist. Bella often felt bad for her parents, especially her mom. She made a mental note to reach out to her twin.

Without any further conversation about her absent sister, Bella and her parents enjoyed a delicious meal. After dinner, they relaxed and drank beer in the family room. Full and comfortable, Bella relaxed on the sofa. She had no desire to move, but she began the notice lustful glances being exchanged between her parents. Bella stood, ready to leave. She knew exactly what the looks meant. Even after so many years, her parents still couldn't keep their hands off of each other. Bella decided to leave before she got thrown out.

"Sooo, I'm gonna go." Bella chuckled.

She didn't get an argument from either of her parents.

"Ooo-kay," Bella muttered. She grabbed her bag and headed to the door.

"Wait, pumpkin. Let me walk you to the car."

"Daddy, I'm good. You don't have to—"

"Little girl, I said wait," Bill demanded.

Bella did as she was told and stopped at the door. Her dad didn't like to repeat himself, and Bella wasn't about to make him. Winona stood to her feet and walked over. She tucked a strand of hair behind Bella's ear and kissed her cheek.

"Thanks for dinner, Ma."

Winona's smile was warm and motherly. "Thanks for coming," she replied. "I like feeding my babies."

Bella's dad opened the front door and held it open for her to exit.

"I'll see you later, Ma." Bella stepped out on the porch. It was dark and a bit cool outside.

Her dad followed her out and accompanied her to her car. "Pumpkin, I need you to do me a favor."

"Anything, Daddy. What's up?"

"See if you can get in touch with your sister and have her call your mom."

Bella looked up at her dad. He would press for Donna to call home for the sake of their mother, but Bella knew that he wanted to hear from her just as bad as her mom did.

CREED 2
by *Phoenix Daniels*

"I'll do what I can," Bella promised.

Bill kissed the top of Bella's head and opened her car door. Bella climbed in.

"Thank you," he said before closing the door.

Bill stepped back from the curb and waited for Bella to pull off. She wanted to call NiYah to find out if she had discovered something that could help her case, but she knew that he wouldn't go inside until she pulled away from the curb. So, Bella pulled off, deciding to call NiYah when she got home.

*****

Bella's phone was ringing as she entered her small house in the South Shore neighborhood. She had a nice size bedroom and two small guestrooms, one of which she used as a closet slash dressing room. Her kitchen was just big enough for a woman who barely cooked, but she had a large deck in the back. But, to Bella, the best thing about her house was that it was walking distance from the beach. Bella loved living near the water. Every morning, she made it a point to go for either a run or a walk on the beach.

CREED 2
by *Phoenix Daniels*

After fishing the phone out of her pocket, Bella swiped to answer. It was Taylor.

"Hey, Taylor, what's up?"

"Girl…" Taylor sighed.

Bella's antennas rose instantly.

"What's going on?" Bella asked her friend.

"Can you drop by the penthouse tomorrow afternoon? I can explain then."

"Yeah, but is everything okay?"

"Yeah, yeah. I'm cool, I guess. I'll see you tomorrow?"

Taylor seemed upset, but she didn't seem to be in a panic. So, Bella agreed to meet up with her the next day and ended the call. She tossed her phone on the cocktail table and went into the kitchen. After pouring herself a glass of wine, Bella washed the dishes that she'd left in the sink the night before. Then she shook her head, thinking that surely, she would be a better housekeeper if she didn't work so many hours a day.

After cleaning the kitchen, Bella grabbed a glass, the bottle of wine, and headed toward her bedroom. She hadn't gotten one foot across the threshold to her peaceful place when she heard the lock to her back-door turn. Bella paused for a few seconds, but she wasn't concerned. She knew exactly who was entering her house. She sat the bottle and glass on an end table, next to her recliner.

"Hey, Bella doll!" Dean shouted from the hallway.

"Hey, bae. I'm in the bedroom!"

Bella kicked off her shoes and plopped down on the recliner. The chair was her favorite spot in her house. She grabbed the remote and turned the television on just as Dean poked his handsome, smiling face through the doorway.

Dean was Bella's ex-husband. But the end of their marriage hadn't ruined their relationship. They were still friends. As a matter of fact, Dean was like her *best* friend.

"I fixed the brakes on your Chevelle."

"My hero," Bella beamed.

Her jet black 1970 Chevelle was her baby.

Dean stepped into the bedroom and walked over to the bed. He turned to sit, but Bella stopped him with a grunt.

"Don't you get on my bed in them street clothes," she warned.

Dean stood upright and lifted an eyebrow at Bella. "Das how you gonna treat me after I labored under your vehicle for hours?"

CREED 2
by *Phoenix Daniels*

"Go get a glass," she urged, ignoring him and gesturing toward the bottle of wine.

As Dean exited the bedroom, Bella took notice of his extremely good looks. That was one thing about him that remained constant. Bella's ex was a tall, bronze Adonis with long African locks. His muscular body was covered with tattoos, giving him the appearance of a dude with hood credibility that he didn't have. Dean was a lawyer. Granted, he was no punk, but he didn't have a thuggish bone in his body.

Bella filled her glass with wine, knocked it back, and then refilled it. She took a sip from the glass and placed it on the end table. Dean entered the room and held his glass out to Bella.

"How was dinner?" he asked as she poured.

"My mom made Hunter's Stew and fried, green tomatoes."

"Mm-mm…and you didn't bring me any?" Dean complained.

"How was I supposed to know you were gonna be here?"

Dean narrowed his eyes and took a sip of the red wine. "You should have guessed."

"They asked about you."

CREED 2
by *Phoenix Daniels*

Dean sighed and sat on the floor. He rested his back against the bed. Even though Bella couldn't see his face, she could feel his anguish.

"Have you told them yet?" he asked.

"Dean, we've been divorced for five years. Why is it so important to you that they know?"

Dean scratched his scalp and blew out a frustrated breath. "Because I still consider them family, Bella. They deserve the truth. I agreed to let you handle things your way, but I don't think you'll ever tell them the truth. Are you that ashamed of me?"

The sadness in Dean's voice made Bella feel like shit. She slid down on the floor and crawled over to him. Bella placed her head on his shoulder and whispered, "I could *never* be ashamed of you. Other than my dad, you're the most honest and courageous man that I know. I'm just afraid of how my parents will react." Bella placed her hand over his. "I couldn't bear to see you lose another set of parents."

Dean was gay. Bella didn't know that when they were married, and she wasn't sure that Dean knew it either. He had been in denial, fighting his impulses since he was a teenager. He really thought that he could overcome his attraction to men and live a normal life. When he realized that he couldn't pray away his gay, he immediately confessed his urges to Bella. Although she was devastated, she appreciated his honesty.

"Bella, it's taken me a long time to get to the point in my life where I can love and accept who I am. If your parents can't continue to love me once they find out who I am, I'll have to live with that. I will be sad, but I'll survive."

"I know, Bella," acknowledged in a sad tone. "I just don't want to see you go through what you went through when you came out to your parents."

Bella knew that Dean still felt the pain of his parents disowning him. She remembered the rage that she'd felt toward them when they told their only son that he was dead to them.

Dean wrapped his arm around Bella and pulled her head to his chest. "Don't worry so much, Bell. I can deal with anything as long as I have you," Dean assured.

Bella held him tight. "You'll always have me," she promised. "I love you, friend."

Dean kissed Bella's forehead. "And I love you, Bella doll."

CHAPTER FIVE

LUCAS

Lucas stepped off the elevator and walked toward Victor's penthouse apartment. He was greeted by Gregor.

"What's up, big guy?" Lucas greeted, even though he was almost as big as the bodyguard.

"Same song, different key. How are you, Mr. Creed?"

"Lucas. Please call me Lucas."

Even though Gregor nodded, Lucas knew that he wouldn't comply. He'd insisted on the informal greeting many times before. Lucas just shook his head and chuckled as he entered his brother's apartment. He crossed the foyer and walked straight to the bar.

"Victor!" he called out as he poured himself a glass of cognac.

"You need a bullhorn?" Victor grumbled as he entered the room.

"Naw, I got the result that I was looking for. What's up, bro. Why I have I been summoned?"

CREED 2
by Phoenix Daniels

Before Victor could respond, his brother's fiancée entered the room. She walked over to give him a hug.

"Hello, beautiful."

"Hey, Lucas. Thanks for coming."

"Anything for you," Lucas responded with a mischievous grin.

He knew all too well just how possessive his big brother could be over his fiancée. And Lucas couldn't blame him. Taylor was a drop-dead gorgeous, powerhouse of a woman. She was tough, intelligent, funny, and built like a goddess. Lucas respected his big brother and his relationship with Taylor, but no heterosexual male could help himself from admiring her curves for a second or two. And admiring was exactly what he was doing until Victor slapped him upside his head.

"What the fuck?!" Lucas barked. His natural reaction would have been to knock the shit out of his brother, but he restrained himself. "Keep your fucking hands to yourself!" Lucas barked.

"Keep your fucking *eyes* to yourself!" Victor retorted.

"I didn't—"

"I see nothing's changed around here."

CREED 2
by *Phoenix Daniels*

Lucas was interrupted by an amused female voice from behind. He turned toward the source and lost his footing when he realized that the voice had come from his dead sister-in-law. "What the…how…how can this be?" he stammered.

"Divine intervention," Rosemary jested.

She walked over and gave Lucas a hug, but he was too shocked to return her affection. It wasn't that he wasn't happy to see her alive. He was simply stunned by her presence. Lucas stepped back and grabbed her by the shoulders. He stared deep into Rosemary's blue eyes. Lucas needed to make sure that he wasn't imagining her presence. Once he was satisfied that she was real, Lucas pulled her into his arms and hugged her tight. He was aware that she and Victor had never loved each other the way a married couple should have, but he'd always liked Rosemary.

Lucas stepped back and turned to Victor.

"What's going on?" he asked.

"It's a long story," Victor responded in a weary tone. "Let's talk about it over lunch."

Lucas nodded and followed his brother into the dining room. There was never a dull moment in the life of a Creed.

BELLA

Bella stepped out of the elevator and ran smack into a giant man wall. She stumbled backward, but the giant grabbed her elbows, keeping her steady on her feet.

"I'm sorry, ma'am. I was just—"

"It's fine. I'm fine. I'm here to see the governor."

"Right this way, Detective."

Gregor released Bella's elbow and escorted her to Victor's apartment. He opened the door and ushered her inside.

"The governor is expecting you, but I need your weapon."

Bella rolled her eyes. "Yeah, right, big fella," she scoffed.

She went to walk away, but the big man grabbed her arm. Bella's eyes landed on the large hand on her arm and then back to his face.

"You need to get your hand off me," Bella warned through gritted teeth.

"Detective, I'm only doing my job. I need you to turn over your firearm."

Bella inhaled a calming breath. She didn't like being manhandled.

"It's okay, Gregor," Victor interrupted. "I'm almost sure that the detective is not here to kill me."

Bella could tell that he wasn't happy about it, but Gregor nodded and released her arm.

"This way, detective," Victor offered, as he walked across the foyer.

Bella followed Victor through the large penthouse and into what she guessed was the entertainment room.

"Hey, friend," Taylor greeted when she entered.

Bella didn't recognize the woman sitting on the sofa, but she immediately recognized Victor's fine-as-fuck little brother, Lucas. If she were to be honest, Bella had never been attracted to men of other races. But Lucas was a white boy that demanded a double take.

"Wassup?" Bella greeted, trying not to stare at the tall, green-eyed, hunk.

"Ooh... she's pretty," crooned the blonde woman. "Lucas, isn't she beautiful?"

She stood and walked closer. Bella folded her arms and narrowed her eyes as the woman looked her up and down in assessment.

"You're Indian," she guessed. "Native American or from Asian Indian?"

"It's essentially the same thing," Bella muttered, rolling her eyes.

She looked over at Taylor and gave her the, '*Who the fuck is this bitch?*' look.

Taylor shrugged and gestured toward the bar. "Drink?" she asked.

"Naw, I'm still on the clock. What's up?"

Bella watched as Victor made his way to the bar. He poured brown liquor into a glass and consumed it in one gulp. Bella blew out a harsh breath. She was becoming impatient.

"Meet Rosemary Creed," Taylor finally offered.

Bella turned to the blonde and waited for someone to get to the point. "Oo-kay?"

"Rosemary is Victor's wife," Taylor revealed.

Confusion caused Bella's brow to wrinkle. She was positive that the governor's wife was dead. "*His wife?* I thought—"

"We all did," chimed Lucas. "Apparently, we are witnessing a miracle."

"I don't understand," Bella admitted, looking to Victor for an explanation.

"Well, it seems that—"

"I faked my death," Rosemary blurted out, cutting Taylor off.

LUCAS

Unable to look away, Lucas stared unabashedly at the detective. The woman was blindingly beautiful. Her jet black hair flowed like liquid satin. She was tall and lean with legs that seemed to go on forever. Yet, she was still curvy enough to stiffen Lucas' cock. Because of her strong Indian features, he was sure that she was Native American.

Confusion etched her beautiful face as Rosemary explained why she had faked her death.

"You paying attention?" Victor asked in a hushed tone.

"Captivated," Lucas muttered, never taking his eyes off of the detective.

She graced him with a glance, before blinking nervously and looking away. It was in that moment that Lucas knew he had gotten her attention.

They had met before, and he remembered the way she had looked at him. She pretended to be uninterested, but Lucas was no fool. He knew when a woman was attracted to him. He'd seen the look of desire glowing in the eyes of many women, young and old. But Lucas would wait patiently until Rosemary was done with her outlandish tale to make his move.

Since he'd heard Rosemary's story, just before the detective arrived, Lucas excused himself from the room. He went into the kitchen and grabbed a bottle of spring water from the fridge. What he truly wanted was a two-finger pour of Victor's good bourbon, but it was still morning. So, he settled.

"Is there something that I can get for you?" a feminine voice asked from behind.

Lucas turned to find a petite woman that was maybe in her early thirties standing behind him. He hadn't heard her walk up. Lucas twisted the cap from the water bottle and asked, "Who are you?"

"I'm Vera, the new housekeeper," she replied. She smiled and added, "I'm willing to bet that you are one of the governor's brothers."

"And you would win that bet, Vera. Lucas Creed. It's nice to meet you."

"It's nice to meet you," she responded softly.

Lucas noticed that the housekeeper was blushing. She was an attractive woman with palm-sized breasts. And her face was displaying the very look of desire that Lucas had become accustomed to.

"Mr. Creed, is there anything I can get for you?" she repeated.

"I'm gonna think on it and let you know later," Lucas responded in a drawl that he knew would make her respond.

Vera definitely deserved a second look, but she was nothing like the goddess that was in his brother's den.

But he flirted anyway.

CHAPTER SIX

TAYLOR

Taylor watched as Bella's expression changed when Lucas reentered the den. She was clearly attracted to him. That was obvious. But what was amusing to Taylor was that she seemed to be irritated by the fact that she found him attractive. Bella put forth great effort not to look in his direction. And in her struggle to ignore Lucas, she'd become downright fidgety.

"As horribly twisted as this story is, what does it have to do with *me*?" Bella shot at Taylor.

Taylor wanted to roll her eyes at her cranky friend. Since she'd known Bella, she had always been brash and rough around the edges. But she was also sweet and thoughtful.

"You're working Collier's case, right?" Taylor asked with a bit of irritation of her own.

She was in a pissy mood too. Shit, her fiancé's wife did just rise from the fucking dead.

"I am," Bella confirmed.

Taylor turned to Rosemary. "Tell her," she urged.

"You mean to tell me that as long as this damn story took, you haven't told me everything?"

Taylor blew out a harsh breath and turned to her bitchy friend. "Would you shut the fuck up," she gritted.

"You shut up, heffa. Tell me what?" Bella turned to Rosemary, wondering why she was being so theatrical. She wished she'd just spit the shit out.

"It's simple. The woman who tried to kill me said that she had found out where I was by torturing Collier. You find her, you'll close your case."

BELLA

Bella tilted her head and glared at Victor's wife. She was standing across from her with her arms folded and a look of satisfaction on her face that she hadn't earned. One would think that she had found the Lindbergh baby.

"Well, okay, Mrs. Creed. Tell me who the woman is so that I can close my investigation."

"I don't know who she is. I had never seen the woman a day in my life until she kidnapped me."

Bella looked over at Taylor who only shrugged. Taylor understood that the information that Rosemary Creed had just given Bella was almost useless. In fact, not only had she not helped her get any closer to closing the investigation into Collier's death, but she'd just basically dropped another case in her lap. However, Bella did have to wonder if Rosemary's encounter with human traffickers was somehow related to the three dead women in the basement.

After taking a few notes and telling Rosemary to stay in town, Bella prepared to leave. She had to get back to the station because she still needed to comb through hours and hours of video footage from every camera in the hospital.

Bella could feel the heat on the side of her face from Lucas' intense gaze. He'd been staring at her since he returned to the room. The way her body was reacting to his presence was unnerving. Her skin tingled and her nipples hardened almost painfully when Lucas was close. From feet away, Bella could smell the masculine scent of oak and Egyptian musk that set Lucas apart from Victor's scent of mint and power.

When Lucas left the den, she felt a sense of relief. But, surprisingly, she also felt a sense of loss. She hadn't been so attracted to a man since Dean. Her body hadn't reacted so strongly to a man's presence since Dean either.

Bella tucked her notebook in her back pocket and walked over to Taylor. To most, she may have looked cool and confident. And, despite how hot and bothered Lucas was making her, Bella did her best to keep it that way.

"Is there someplace we can talk?" Bella asked.

Taylor nodded her head and walked toward the door. Bella followed her out of the den and into the hall. They walked down a hall that was way too big to be in an apartment until they reached a closed door.

CREED 2
by *Phoenix Daniels*

"Dayyyum," Bella crooned when they entered the massive bedroom.

If she were to be honest, Bella had never in her life seen a bedroom so beautiful. Everything from the walls to the carpet and comforter was white. But the crisp white was accented with very contrasting crimson accessories.

"Yeah, the other half," Taylor quipped. "What's up?"

Bella grabbed Taylor's hand and led her to a white loveseat, adorned with crimson pillows. She pulled Taylor to sit with her and looked her in the eye.

"Are you okay?"

Taylor closed her eyes, fell back on the loveseat, and blew out a heavy breath. "No," she admitted. "Bella, I am *not* okay."

Taylor opened her eyes. They were filled with moisture. Bella squeezed Taylor's hand and pulled her head onto her shoulder. "Taylor, Victor loves you. That's indisputable. That man loves you."

Taylor used her free hand to wipe tears from her cheek. "I know he loves me, but…"

"But what?"

"He's married to her. He says that they got married for appearances. Supposedly, to further his political career."

"And? He's governor now. He doesn't need her. His approval rate has climbed considerably since he's been with you."

"Yeah, so, how's he gonna spin the return of his dead wife and his engagement to me. If he divorces her and marries me, the press is going to demonize him." Taylor hiccupped as more tears fell from her eyes.

"Taylor, why don't you let him worry about that? I believe that the governor would move mountains to be with you. And I don't doubt for one minute that he can handle the press." Bella gave Taylor's shoulder a reassuring squeeze. "Trust your man, baby. I trust him. And you know that I don't trust no damn body."

Taylor chuckled and sat up straight. She wiped her eyes and nodded. "You're right." She sniffed. "Victor will take care of things. That's what he does."

Taylor got up from the loveseat and walked into the bathroom. Bella could hear running water. So, she assumed that Taylor was watching her face.

CREED 2
by *Phoenix Daniels*

"So, what's up with you and Lucas?" Taylor called out from the bathroom.

"What? Nothing. What do you mean?"

Taylor reentered the bedroom with the look of skepticism. "Cow, don't play games with me. You are clearly into that man, and his eyes never left you."

"Girl, please," Bella scoffed. "I ain't thinking about that man."

Taylor flopped down next to her friend. "Bella, you ain't thought about no man since you and Dean split up. Why? Are you still in love with Dean? Because, if you—"

"I'm not in love with Dean, Tay," Bella interrupted in a frustrated tone. "I just don't want your soon-to-be brother-in-law."

Taylor narrowed her eyes as if she were trying to see into Bella's brain. "You still got a thing against dating white guys, don't you?"

Bella rolled her eyes, wishing that Taylor would just let it go and mind her own business. She stood from the loveseat and walked toward the door. "I gotta go. Gotta get back to the station," Bella muttered as she left the room.

She stepped into the hall, and of course, she found herself face to face with Lucas Creed. Her steps halted, and her heart pounded erratically in her chest. Lucas Creed was knee-buckling fine. His hair was dark like Victor's and his eyes were green just like his, but whereas his older brother was politically polished, Lucas was rough around the edges. He had a major I-don't-give-a-fuck air about him.

Lucas was tall and solid. Beyond his black V-neck, Bella could see that he had the form of a man that spent time in the gym religiously. His thick, chin-length hair bounced freely around his handsome face, and his full lips encased perfect white teeth.

Lucas was watching Bella in a way that made her nervous. She had seen a lot in her thirty-six years on earth, and there wasn't much that made her nervous.

"Detective, it's good to see you again."

Ooh!

His voice was like cool silk, rubbing against her warm naked skin. Bella cleared her throat and forced herself to behave like she would if she weren't standing in front of Adonis.

"Nice to see you, Mr. Creed," she muttered as she walked past him.

Lucas grabbed her arm. Bella's breath hitched when a current of *something* traveled throughout her entire body. She pulled out of his grasp and glared up at him.

"May I walk you out?" he asked before Bella could chastise him.

"Why?"

"I'd like a word."

"Alright." Bella sighed.

Together, they continued down the hall. Bella simply could not understand why she was so uncomfortable. It's not like she had never been around a good-looking man before. They rounded the corner and entered the large living room. After they crossed the foyer, Bella turned to Lucas. She was immediately startled by how close he was standing to her.

Bella cleared her throat nervously and asked, "Mr. Creed, what did you want to discuss?"

Bella's heart raced when he slapped her with a disarming grin. "I'm going to call you Bella because it defines you. So, I'd like it if you would call me Lucas."

His voice, his scent, his nearness caused Bella to quiver. "Fine," was all she could manage.

"I'd like you to have dinner with me."

CREED 2
by *Phoenix Daniels*

"I don't think so."

Lucas' brows bunched. Bella imagined that a man like him wasn't at all accustomed to being rejected. The thought empowered Bella enough to regain some semblance of control of herself.

"Why, Bella? Do you not think that I'm attractive?"

Bella reached for the doorknob, but Lucas covered her hand. Any bit of control that she thought that she'd regained suddenly fled.

He pulled her to face him. "I asked you a question, Beauty."

Bella looked up, and despite staring into his hypnotic, green eyes, she managed to strengthen her resolve. "I'm just not interested, Mr. Creed."

With that said, Bella escaped his grasp, opened the door, and left the penthouse. Once she was in the hall, she wondered if she had just won something or lost something.

CHAPTER SEVEN

BELLA

Bella walked up to the elaborate Gold Coast townhouse and jogged up the steps. She had made several attempts to contact Kara Edwards. Since Rosemary mentioned that she was involved with Collier, and had a part in Taylor's shooting, Bella had wanted to bring Kara in for questioning. But after several attempts, it became clear to her that Ms. Edwards was avoiding her.

Bella rang the doorbell and knocked on the fancy, French doors. After a minute or so, she was sure that Kara wasn't coming to the door. Bella turned to walk away, thinking that she would have to show Kara Edwards that she wasn't playing games with her. But, just as she was about to go down the stairs, the front door flew open.

An irritated, "What?" came from the doorway.

Bella turned toward the door and came face to face with the very woman that she'd wanted to see. "Kara Edwards?" Bella asked, even though she already knew who she was.

"Yes."

CREED 2
by *Phoenix Daniels*

"Miss Edwards, I'm Detective Devereaux from the Chicago Police Department. I'd appreciate a moment of your time."

Bella noticed the instant change in Miss Edwards' demeanor as soon as she announced her office. It went from irritation to anxiety. "May I come in?" Bella asked, even though she was already stepping through the door.

"Sure... yes. P-please, come in, Detective."

"Thank you," Bella replied as she stepped past Kara.

As she walked across the vestibule, Bella marveled at the elegance of Victor's former press secretary's townhome. If nothing else, the woman had style.

Kara walked ahead of Bella. "Right this way, detective."

Bella followed Kara into an office. When she hurried around a large desk and sat, Bella knew that Kara was attempting to assert her authority. That was obvious. It was a ploy, but a ploy that worked on most. It was the very reason why Bella preferred to conduct her interviews in the police station. But since she couldn't, she chose to remain standing.

"Miss Edwards, it has come to my attention that you and Collier Sanders were close."

Bella watched Kara's reaction while she waited for an answer.

"Yes, I was familiar with Collier. We both worked for the governor."

Bella smiled and stuffed her hands into the pockets of her slacks. "Now, Miss Edwards, I didn't ask if you were familiar. I asked if you were close."

Anxiety flashed in Kara's eyes for fraction of a second. "No, Detective, Collier and I were not close. He had a job to do, and so did I."

"Did you speak to him the night of his death?"

Without the slightest hesitation, Kara responded, "No."

"Miss Edwards, had you spoken to Collier Sanders the night that Officer Taylor Montgomery was shot?"

Before she could stop herself, Kara frowned at the mention of Taylor's name. "No, I did not, Detective. What is all this about?"

Bella could see rays of annoyance emanating from the woman. She was obviously bothered by the fact that Bella was questioning her. But Bella couldn't give zero fucks.

CREED 2
by *Phoenix Daniels*

"Again, Miss Edwards, did you speak to Collier Sanders either the night of Taylor's shooting or the night of Collier's death?"

Kara stood from her chair. The tips of her fingers were turning white from pressing them aggressively into her desk. "I said, no," she responded in a slightly elevated tenor.

"Cell phone records say otherwise," Bella calmly revealed.

Kara walked from around the over-sized desk and gestured toward the door. "I think it's time for you to leave, Detective."

Bella nodded in agreement and walked toward the door. She turned to Kara, and just before walking out, she said, "I'll be taking your official statement tomorrow morning at nine o'clock. Don't show, and there'll be a warrant issued for your arrest."

"I'll bring my attorney," Kara snarled.

"That's a good idea, Miss Edwards," Bella shot back as she exited Kara's home office.

CREED 2
by *Phoenix Daniels*

*****

Bella rubbed her eyes and leaned back in the office
chair. She was sitting in the audio-visual center of the
detective's division, which would better be described as a tiny
office. She was painfully combing through hospital surveillance
video from the night Collier Sanders was murder.

"Ugh!"

Bella frustrated grunt bounced off the walls in the tiny
room. She was ready to give up and call it a night when
something on the video caused her to move closer to the screen.
Bella squinted at the footage of the hallway that led to Collier's
hospital room. She could make out what looked to be a nurse
entering her victim's room.

Bella looked at the time stamp, which indicated that it
was 3:37 AM. But the early morning visit by a nurse wasn't
what got her attention. Nurses checking on patients in the
middle of the night was common in any hospital. It was the fact
that the nurse was wearing what looked like motorcycle boots
that captured Bella's attention.

The video wasn't very clear, but the nurse appeared to
be a slim and female. Her hair was dark, but she couldn't see

the nurses face. She seemed to be aware of the cameras and avoiding them.

The nurse entered Collier's room. According to the video, she stayed for exactly four minutes before exiting and leaving in the opposite direction of the camera.

Bella pulled the disc out of the player and put it to the side. She wasn't at all surprised that it only took four minutes to kill Collier. He was, after all, immobile. She slid in another disc, which was footage from the camera at the opposite end of the hall.

Bella barely blinked as she stared at the screen, looking for a good image of the woman who had entered Collier's room. Once she found the only workable image, she pulled it from the DVD player and put it with the other CD. Bella leaned over and grabbed the office phone. She dialed the inter-department number for the video tech.

"Tech services. This is Bruce."

"Bruce, it's Bella Devereaux. How are you?"

Bella could hear Bruce blow out a frustrated breath through the receiver. He clearly wasn't happy to hear from her. Bruce had started out courteous and helpful until Bella turned him down after he invited her to dinner.

CREED 2
by *Phoenix Daniels*

"What can I do for you, Detective?" he asked in a bored tone.

"I caught a case with video. Can you see if you can clean it up for me?"

"I got a few jobs ahead of you. I don't know when I'll be able to get to you."

Lies!

Bella was no fool. She knew that Bruce wasn't doing shit in that office but eating and watching porn on his phone. "Bruce, this case is involving the man who shot Taylor Montgomery. It takes precedence."

"Says who?" he asked arrogantly.

Bella groaned. Bruce was behaving like a child. Why couldn't he just do his fucking job?

"I'll tell you what, Bruce. I'll just call the governor and tell him that you said fuck his fiancée."

"Send it over!" Bruce snapped before hanging up on Bella.

Bella placed the phone on the receiver and shook her head. Taylor was a fellow police officer. She shouldn't have had to drop the governor's name to get Bruce to do his job. It's a damn shame.

CREED 2
by *Phoenix Daniels*

Men!

They were nothing but big-ass male babies.

CHAPTER EIGHT
VICTOR

Victor placed a glass of red wine down on the table next to Taylor's plate. They were sitting down for dinner. But dinner wasn't exactly festive. It hadn't been since Rosemary had invaded their lives. For an entire week, the tension between him and Taylor could've been cut with a chainsaw. He had tried many times to convince Taylor that he wasn't in love with Rosemary. Taylor always said that she believed him, but things just weren't the same. Victor placed his own wineglass on the table and sat in the chair next to Taylor. He grabbed her hand and pulled it to his lips. "We need to talk," Victor told her.

Although Taylor hadn't been very talkative as of late, Victor was determined to make things right with his woman.

Taylor turned in his direction. She looked tired like she hadn't been sleeping, which meant that she was lying next to him pretending to be asleep,

"Not now, Victor." Taylor sighed. "I know that we have to talk, but can we do it later?"

The sad and worried look in her eyes broke Victor's heart. He had vowed to himself and to Taylor that he would never hurt her. Even though he'd had no hand in Rosemary's decision to fake her death nor her return, Victor still felt responsible for the fact that Taylor was in pain.

"Alright, sweetheart. We can talk later," he conceded.

He didn't want to add to Taylor's stress so he finished his meal in silence. When he was done, he walked into Taylor's kitchen and put his plate and fork in the dishwasher.

"I'm going to bed," he called out from the kitchen.

When Taylor didn't answer, he went into the bedroom and pulled a pair of boxers out of the drawer that she'd assigned him. Frustrated and on the verge of anger, Victor walked across the room and plopped down on the bed. He groaned out loud and dropped his face in his hands. Victor simply didn't know what else to do or say to convince Taylor that he was dangerously in love with her and he had no intention of navigating life without her.

Victor stood and walked into the master bathroom. In the shower, he would figure out a way to convince Taylor that everything was going to be okay.

TAYLOR

Victor walked out of the bathroom just as Taylor entered her bedroom. She paused at the sight of him. He was so beautifully masculine. He was still a bit wet with a towel wrapped around his waist. Little beads of water dripped down his muscular torso to the V that disappeared into his towel. His wet, dark hair was slicked back, exposing even more of his handsome face.

Maybe she wasn't being rational, but the thought of losing the man she loved so very much was ripping her apart from the inside. Taylor's head fell. Her entire body tensed up when Victor crossed the room in three giant steps and grabbed her by her shoulders.

"Taylor, sweetheart, you're killing me," he whispered painfully. "I love you so much, baby."

Without looking at him, Taylor whispered, "I know you do, Victor."

Victor gently squeezed her shoulders. "Look at me," he prompted. When Taylor didn't respond, his voice became more forceful. "Look at me, Taylor!"

Taylor tore her eyes away from his chest and reluctantly, look into his eyes.

"Have I ever lied to you?"

"No," Taylor responded with a weak voice.

"Ever? Even once?" Victor prodded.

"No," Taylor said, shaking her head.

"Then why don't you trust me?"

Taylor could see the pain in his eyes. His voice was filled with agony. Suddenly, not trusting Victor seemed like a betrayal. "I do trust you, Victor." Taylor sighed.

"Then why have you turned away from me? You've denied me the affection that I need from the woman I love. I didn't do this, babe."

Tears welled up in Taylor's eyes. Victor was right. He didn't create the situation. And he was just as affected, if not more, by Rosemary's return.

"I'm sorry," Taylor whimpered. "I'm so sorry. I know it's not your fault."

Victor pulled Taylor into his arms. She wrapped her arms around him and placed her hands on his broad back. Her fingers dipped into sinewy muscles as they slid across his back.

"Don't you wanna marry me, sweetheart? Don't you wanna be my wife?"

"Yes, baby. Of course, I want to marry you. I love you," Taylor professed.

"That's good because you already said yes, and I have no plans on letting you change your mind."

Taylor's head relaxed against his wide chest and inhaled his fresh scent. He rubbed her back gently as he held her tight. The sound of his heartbeat coordinated with the beat of hers.

"Victor, bae, I was just feeling insecure," Taylor admitted.

Victor eased her off of his chest and cupped her face in his hands. He forced her to look up at him and into his beautiful green eyes.

"Hear me, Taylor. There is no woman that has *ever* walked the face of this earth that should cause you to be insecure. There isn't a word in any language that could describe what you mean to me. I *fucking* love you. And I ain't livin' without you."

Speechless from his declaration, Taylor smiled and nodded her head. Victor pulled her face to his and pressed his lips to hers. Taylor tightened her grip on his back and moaned when Victor slipped his tongue between her lips and deepened the kiss. As they made love with their mouths, Victor removed his hands from Taylor's face and wrapped his arm around her waist. With his other hand, he cupped her butt and lifted her off of her feet. Taylor wrapped her legs around Victor's waist and pushed her eager center against his hard dick. She rubbed against him, causing his towel to fall to the floor. Knowing that Victor was in his beautifully naked glory, pushed Taylor to the brink of frenzy. She loved Victor, needed him. She needed to feel his love from the inside out. Taylor held on tight as Victor carried her across the room. He placed her on the bed and undressed her slowly. Reverently, Victor worshiped her entire body for most of the night.

CHAPTER NINE

BELLA

Bella pulled to the curb in front of Kara Edward's house. It was 3:45 in the afternoon and Bella hadn't heard a word from her. She'd tried several times to reach her by phone, but she was unsuccessful. The woman had a knack for blowing Bella off. A squad car occupied by two uniformed officers pulled behind her. She stepped out of her unmarked Chevy and walked toward Kara's townhouse. She had been able to secure the warrant for her arrest based on Kara's cell phone records, a combination of her own false statements, and hearsay statements from a confidential informant—Rosemary.

With the uniformed officers behind her, Bella jogged up the steps. As she reached the landing, Bella could see that one of the French doors was open. She and the officers shared a look before approaching the door. Bella knocked hard and called out Kara's name. When there was no answer, she stepped inside the townhouse. She eased her .45 out of its holster and began to search the house. One of the officers veered toward the living room. The other headed up the stairs. Bella crept, weapon drawn, down the main hall. She took quiet, careful steps to the kitchen where she found nothing. Then she turned and headed back down the hall. There were two closed doors. She slowly opened the first door. It was the hall closet. Bella cleared it, closed it, and walked toward the second door. Since she'd been at the house the day before, Bella knew that room to be Kara's office. Still holding her pistol, Bella turned the knob and stepped inside Kara's office.

The search for Kara was over.

Bella gasped in horror at the gruesome scene. She inhaled a deep breath and blew it out while struggling to hold on to her lunch. The carnage before her was ungodly. It was an absolute bloodbath. There was blood covering almost every inch of the office. Kara's bloody body was lying on the desk. She would've been facing the ceiling *if* she'd had a head. Her head had been completely severed from her body and placed on top of her stomach. It had been positioned to face whoever entered the room.

"Oh, shit!" exclaimed one of the officers behind her.

Bella groaned and pulled her radio out of her back pocket. She placed it to her mouth and pressed the key. "5813," she announced into the radio.

"Go ahead, 5813," the dispatcher prompted.

"Oh, my God," mumbled the other officer as he did the sign of the cross.

Bella turned from the officer and spoke into the radio. "Squad, I got 110 at 1301 North State Parkway."

"5813, do you need me to roll you an ambulance just to be sure?"

"There is no need for an ambulance, squad. Please notify the coroner, the crime lab, and my supervisor. I believe her beat number is 5810."

"10-4, 5813. You okay? You need backup?" the dispatcher asked.

"Naw, I got a beat car on scene. But can you roll me a couple of cars to secure the crime scene."

"10-4, 5813. Stand by."

Bella stuffed the radio back inside her pocket and looked up to the ceiling.

"*Fuck!*" she shouted, furious that she'd just caught another goddamned homicide.

CREED 2
by *Phoenix Daniels*

*****

After several calls, Bella was finally able to get in contact with Taylor. She was hoping that Taylor was home, but of course, she wasn't. So, Bella found herself riding the elevator to Victor's apartment in Storm Tower. It had been a week since she'd seen Victor's brother and she didn't feel like fighting with her feminine parts like she always did whenever he was near.

For the life of her, Bella couldn't understand why her blood heated, her skin tingled, and her pussy throbbed every time Lucas was in the room. The last time he was near, her nipples stayed hard from the warmth of his suggestive gaze.

Bella took a breath and wiped all thoughts of Lucas Creed from her head. Truthfully, folks were dropping like flies around her. She had too much shit to do to be worried about a man who she had no possible future with.

"Hello, Detective," Gregor greeted.

"Hello. Taylor and the governor are expecting me."

"I'm aware of that, Detective. I need to hold your weapon."

"Ugh!" Bella grumbled, rolling her eyes. "Look, dude, Governor Creed has already allowed me to keep my weapon in his presence before."

"Yes, but, that was before we had a discussion that culminated in the governor allowing me to do my job. Now, you are more than welcome to enter, but not with a weapon."

"Look, Gregor. Your name *is* Gregor, right?"

"It is," Gregor responded with a nod.

"Well, Gregor, I'm on duty. It's my right to hold on to my weapon."

"You do have the right to bear arms, but not *here*. Let me ask you a question, Bella. It is *Bella*, right."

Awe, okay.

"Yes, my name is Bella."

"When you go to court and you're on duty, are you allowed take your weapon inside the courtroom?"

Bella knew exactly where he was going with the question. "No," she admitted.

"Well, this is the home of the governor of Illinois, and you will show him the same respect. Now, I need your weapon."

CREED 2
by Phoenix Daniels

The giant had a point, and Bella didn't have time to stand in the hall and argue with him. She pulled her .45 out of the holster and handed it to him by the handle. She moved to step inside, but his large body blocked the doorway.

"What?" Bella breathed.

"Your backup gun too."

Bella rolled her eyes and bent down to pull her .38 out of her ankle holster. She huffed and handed him her backup piece.

"Thank you, Detective. I really appreciate your cooperation."

"Yeah, yeah… Can I go inside now?"

"Of course. Taylor and the governor are waiting in the den."

Bella stepped inside once Gregor removed himself from her path. She walked through the large apartment and inhaled the scent of lavender, vanilla, and *money*. Taylor had hit the jackpot with the governor. He was smart, rich, and fine as fuck. But, for that matter, so was his brother. Lucas was all those things, and Bella was avoiding him. And she would continue to do so. Men like Lucas had everything; looks, charm, education, and revenue. They were accustomed to getting anything that they wanted, especially *women*. It was Bella's belief that when a man could have any woman he wanted, he would seldom cherish them once he conquered them. With Victor, Taylor had just gotten lucky. Bella wasn't that lucky, and she wasn't about to be some rich playboy's booty call.

Bella rounded the corner and continued down the hall. The door to the den was open, so she walked in. Neither Taylor nor Victor noticed that she had entered the room. They were at the bar. Taylor was sitting on a stool and Victor was standing between her legs. They were kissing. Taylor was giggling between kisses. They were really enjoying each other's company. They seemed very much in love.

Bella smiled. Victor and Taylor had obviously worked out their issues regarding the return of Rosemary. Bella was glad to see Taylor happy again. Unfortunately, there was business that needed to be tended to. Bella cleared her throat to get their attention.

"Hey, Bella. What's up?" Taylor called, still smiling.

"Hey," Bella greeted as she approached the bar.

Taylor narrowed her eyes as if she were trying to gauge Bella's demeanor. Victor stepped from between Taylor's legs and adjusted his slacks. Bella did her best not to notice the large, almost intimidating bulge between his thighs. She tried hard not to look…*unsuccessfully*. Taylor tilted her head and frowned at Bella.

"Sorry," Bella mouthed when Victor turned to walk behind the bar.

Bella had apologized, but one would have to be Helen Keller not to have noticed that the governor had a big-ass dick.

"What do you want, Bella?" Taylor asked impatiently.

Bella cleared her throat. "I need to know where the two of you were between 9 o'clock last night and 3:45 this afternoon."

Taylor hopped down from the stool and walked toward Bella. "Why?"

"I just need you both to answer the question."

Taylor walked over to the sofa and sat. Bella watched her eyes to see if she was preparing a lie. But the truth was, if Taylor did lie, Bella would've looked the other way. After all, Kara did try to have her killed. Bella was not there to crucify her friend, but she did need answers.

"Well, last night we were both at my house. You can check with Victor's security detail. And this morning, around 8,

I was at the medical section in headquarters to see about getting reinstated to work. You know I've been off since I got shot."

Bella nodded and turned to Victor. "Well, Taylor just told you where I was last night. And as far as this morning, pick up a newspaper. Reporters have been following me around all day, asking questions about this new beverage tax."

"Yeah, I've been meaning to tell you that that tax is some bullshit," Bella scoffed.

Taylor chuckled. "Bae, Bella's addicted to Pepsi."

"That shit'll kill you," Victor quipped, just before lifting a sifter of cognac to his lips.

Bella shook her head and laughed.

"What's this about, Bella?" Taylor asked.

Bella walked over to the bar where Victor was standing. "Hook a sistah up," she said with a nod toward the cognac.

Victor pulled a glass and poured Bella a drink. She could tell that he was surprised since she'd always turned down offerings of alcohol in the past. "I went to question Kara," Bella told them.

"Oh, and what did that bitch have to say?" Taylor asked with a scowl.

CREED 2
by *Phoenix Daniels*

"Well, the first time I questioned her, she said that she only knew Collier from work. She said that she didn't speak to him the day you were shot or the day he was murdered. I told her that her phone records indicated otherwise. Then blah, blah, blah... She wanted a lawyer. She was supposed to come in this morning, but she didn't show. So, I went out there." Bella took a generous sip of cognac.

"And?" Taylor urged.

"Oh, and when I got there, she was dead."

Taylor's mouth flew open. Bella could tell that she was stunned, not in the least bit sad, but shocked. Taylor had no sympathy for the woman who had solicited her murder.

"Damn, Kara's dead," Victor mused.

"Not just dead but *decapitated*," Bella clarified.

In silence, Taylor walked over to the bar and fixed her own drink "So, you were thinking that we had something to do with cutting off a woman's head?"

"Naw, but I had to ask."

Bella walked over to the sofa and sat. She knocked back the rest of her cognac and pointed her glass in Taylor's direction, indicating that she wanted a refill. Taylor looked at

Bella as if she'd grown a third eye. She grabbed the glass from her hand a stood over her.

"What's gotten into you?" Taylor asked since Bella wasn't known to drink anything stronger than wine.

Bella blew out a harsh breath and leaned back on the sofa. "It's this case," she grumbled. "This fucking case is just getting bigger and bigger. Collier's dead. Kara's dead. And, now, I'm chasing some mystery bitch without one clue as to who the hell she is."

Taylor turned to sit next to Bella on the sofa, but Bella pushed Taylor by the butt, prohibiting her from sitting. Taylor turned to Bella with a questioning glare.

"Heffa, fix my drink," Bella blurted.

Victor laughed and grabbed the glass from Taylor's hand. "I got it."

Taylor narrowed her eyes, daring Bella to stop her, as she made another attempt to sit.

"What's next?" Victor asked.

"Well, the first thing I gotta do is find this mystery woman. Until I find her, I'm dead in the water. Governor, I need to speak with your wife."

"Stop calling her that!" Taylor snapped.

"Sorry," Bella muttered. "But I do need to speak with Rosemary. Is she here?"

"No, she's hiding out at my brother's."

"Which brother?" Bella asked, reciting a silent prayer that the brother that Victor was referring to wasn't *Lucas*.

"Lucas," Taylor practically hummed.

Bella shot Taylor a glare that clearly said, "Shut the fuck up."

Victor, ignoring the exchange between the friends, handed Bella her refilled glass. "I'll give him a call. When do you wanna stop by?"

"Tomorrow morning around 10. Where does he live?"

"Not far. He's on Lake Shore Drive. I'll let him know that you're coming by."

"Thank you, Governor."

"Bella, please call me *Victor*. We should be past formalities by this point."

Bella nodded in agreement and lifted the glass to her lips. Her plan was to knock back the potent brown liquid, but she was starting to feel the effects of the first drink. So, she sipped instead.

Victor walked over to the sofa and kissed Taylor's forehead. "I'm gonna leave you ladies to it. I have some work to do."

Taylor watched Victor with loving eyes as he left the room. Once they were alone, she turned to Bella and asked, "What is your deal?"

"What?"

"Girl, as soon as I mentioned Lucas, you got mad tense. What did that man do to you?"

Bella grimaced. "He didn't do anything to me. I don't even know the man."

"Come on, bitch. Stop playing with me."

"Ugh! Taylor, please, can we just drink and stop talking about your brother-in-law. I'm not interested in him or any other man right now. I got too much on my plate."

Taylor glowered at Bella and let out an irritated huff. "You know what, Bella? I'm tired of this shit!" Taylor exclaimed.

Bella squinted at her friend, trying desperately to figure out why Taylor's demeanor had changed all of a sudden.

"What are you talking about? Tired of what shit?" When Taylor shook her head without responding, Bella pushed. "What shit, Taylor?"

"After all of these years, you have been the most closed-off friend that I've ever had. I have never met a person who barricades their feelings like you do."

"Taylor, what are you talking about?" Bella asked even though she knew exactly what Taylor was talking about.

Undoubtedly, agitated, Taylor rolled her eyes. "Bella, stop!" she snapped.

Bella inhaled a deep breath and leaned back on the sofa. Taylor was right. She was closed off. There were so many things that Bella didn't share with her friend. It wasn't because she didn't trust her. If she had to admit it, Bella was simply embarrassed. She hadn't made the best choices in her life.

"And the fucked up thing is, you expect me to open up to you."

"I'm sorry," Bella apologized. "I know that I haven't exactly been an open book."

"Why? Are we not friends?"

"Of course, we are, Tay. It's just—"

"What? It's just what?"

CREED 2
by *Phoenix Daniels*

Bella closed her eyes tight and inhaled a deep breath. She ran her fingers through her hair and opened her eyes to look at Taylor. "Dean is gay," she blurted out before she could change her mind.

Taylor's brows wrinkled with confusion.

"*Dean*? Your ex-husband, Dean?"

"Yes."

"Wait. What?"

Taylor was as shocked as Bella expected.

"Apparently, he wasn't sure that he was gay until he married me," Bella snorted.

Admittedly, Dean being gay had been a major blow to her ego.

"Oh, Bella, I'm so sorry. I had no idea," Taylor consoled softly.

"Nobody knows," Bella admitted.

"Damn, Bell. Are you sure? I mean you guys were married for like *three years*."

"Am I sure? Of course, I'm sure. He told me. Apparently, he'd been privately fighting this battle with his sexuality for years. He thought that he could make himself *normal*," Bella told her, using air quotes on normal for emphasis.

Taylor placed her hand over Bella's. "I am so sorry. That's fucked up."

"Yeah, but, I'm okay with it now. After the way his parents treated him, I can understand why he tried so hard to be straight."

"What happened?"

Bella shook her head in disgust, thinking about Dean's parents and the way they abandoned their only son. "Girl, they disowned him. His dad told Dean that he was dead to him and they no longer had a son."

Taylor sighed. Like Bella, she had come from a loving family. She probably couldn't imagine a parent that would turn their back on their child. Bella, herself, couldn't believe how Dean's parents had mistreated someone as sweet and loving as their only son. Before they found out he was gay, both would often be caught describing him as the perfect son. Once upon a time, she'd loved Dean's mom and dad, but as of late, Bella couldn't stand the sight of them.

"That is sooo messed up. His parents are going to hell. How is Dean taking it?"

"He's hurt, of course. But he's okay. He's living his truth."

"Good. Dean is a sweetheart, and it seemed like you guys were made for each other. I always wondered why you guys divorced."

"We do belong together," Bella sighed. "He's my best friend, Tay."

Taylor smiled and pulled Bella into a hug. Bella, not really used to a lot of physical contact from someone other than her family, waited for the awkward feeling that she got whenever people touched her. When it didn't come, she wrapped her arms around Taylor and hugged her tight.

CHAPTER TEN

LUCAS

Lucas hurried to the door. When he'd gotten the call from Victor the night before, telling him that the sexy detective was coming to his home, he immediately called his assistant to let her know that he wouldn't be in the office.

Lucas had come in contact with plenty of beautiful women over the years, but the thought of seeing Bella Devereaux had made him hop out of bed like a kid on Christmas morning. For the life of him, Lucas couldn't understand why he got so excited about the prospect of spending time with her. He checked the hall mirror and fixed his hair.

"You're behaving like a fucking teenager," Lucas muttered out loud to himself. He opened the door and peered out at Bella.

Damn, she's hot!

Even dressed in standard attire, consisting of blue jeans and a T-shirt, she was extraordinary. Her ink-black hair was pulled into a ponytail, and her exquisite skin reminded Lucas of

91

CREED 2
by *Phoenix Daniels*

a Caribbean sunset. He was fighting an inner battle to stay focused on Bella's face because the sight of her nipples stretching the thin fabric of her form-fitting T-shirt made his cock push against his zipper.

"Good morning, Detective."

"Good morning. I need to have a word with your houseguest."

Lucas wasn't convinced by Bella's dispassionate tone. The fire in her eyes and her body language was betraying her. She could pretend to be uninterested, but Lucas knew the truth. Bella Devereaux wanted him maybe just as bad as he wanted her…maybe even *more*.

Lucas grinned and stepped out of her path, allowing her entrance to his apartment.

"Come on in. Rosemary will be up soon."

Bella seemed surprised that Rosemary was still asleep, but Lucas wasn't. Rosemary had been through a lot. She was physically and emotionally drained.

"She normally gets up around eleven," Lucas offered. "Come. Follow me. I'll pour you some coffee."

"No, thank you. I'm fine." Bella stood close to the door as if she was afraid to step further into Lucas' domain.

CREED 2
by *Phoenix Daniels*

Lucas chuckled at her reluctance. The woman was definitely stubborn. Lucas placed his hand on the small of her back and nudged her gently in the direction of his kitchen. "Come on, Bella. I'm not gonna bite."

Lucas could sense Bella's hesitation as he led her toward the kitchen. Once inside, he directed her to the island and walked over to the coffee maker. He grabbed a cup from the cupboard and turned to Bella.

"How do you take it?"

"Black," was her simple response.

For now, maybe.

Lucas filled her cup with coffee and turned to Bella with a smirk. "You should try a little *cream*. I bet you'd like it."

The corners of Bella's mouth reluctantly curled into a smile. It was actually the first time that he'd seen her smile. As her face softened, it had an indescribable effect on him.

Lucas filled his own cup and joined Bella. He handed her the cup of black coffee and sat on a stool across from her. He watched curiously as she sipped, wondering why she was dead set against seeing him socially. He wondered if she truly wasn't attracted to him or if she only dated black men. Lucas could only hope that she was open to diversity, especially when it came to relationships.

"Why won't you have dinner with me?" Lucas was done with wondering.

Bella blinked up at him, obviously not expecting such a question to be thrown at her. "What?"

"You heard me, Bella Devereaux. I asked why won't you have dinner with me."

Bella placed her cup on the countertop and pressed her palms flat on the table. "Lucas, I've told you already. I'm not interested in going out with you."

"Why?"

Bella recoiled slightly. Maybe she thought that her stating her lack of interest would be the end of their conversation. She was wrong. "*Why?*" she parroted.

She was stalling, and it amused Lucas. "Why?" he repeated in a cool tone.

"I'm just not."

"Is it because I'm a white guy?"

Bella's eyes widened at Lucas' bold assumption. She stood from the table in feigned offense. But Lucas knew very well that she wasn't offended. She was *nervous*. He stood and walked around the island, closing in on her before she could flee the kitchen. He knew that he was invading her personal space, but that was the point. He heard her breath hitch. Her chest was heaving, and he could practically see her heart pounding behind the snug T-shirt. Bella was anything but uninterested. Her erect nipples alone told Lucas so.

Lucas, no longer restraining himself, did what he'd wanted to do ever since he'd laid eyes on her. He slipped his fingers through the dark tresses of her hair, pressed his fingers to her scalp and guided her head until she was looking him in the eye. He placed his lips within an inch of hers and asked, "Why do you lie? Is it an attempt to deceive me or you?"

Bella's lips quivered as if she were attempting to speak, but Lucas wasn't about to allow her to rebuff his advances. She would erase the progress that he felt he had made. Before she could utter a single word, Lucas pushed his lips to hers. He placed his hand on the small of her back as the other massaged her scalp. Bella parted her lips, allowing him entry. Her lips were soft. And, *goddamn*, her softness melted against his hardness. Her kiss was sweet indeed but filled with a hint of desperation. Bella Devereaux needed to be fucked like there was no tomorrow. There was a hunger in her that needed to be fed. Her entire body longed to be worshiped. And Lucas was just the man for that job. He would be sure to manage every inch of her inside and out, from head to toe.

Bella clutched his shoulders and moaned into his mouth, sending radiant vibrations directly to his throbbing cock. Lucas was painfully erect, and all he could think about was being balls-deep in Bella's heat. He gripped her by the ass and pulled her into his hard-on. She needed to know what she was doing to him. He could feel her heartbeat and he knew that if he could feel hers, she could feel his racing heart too. Lucas was all too ready to toss her on the counter and lick her sweet pussy until she begged for his cock. And he had decided that he was going to do just that, but the sound of the refrigerator opening caused Bella to freeze.

Fuck!

Bella ripped her lips from his, and Lucas had never felt such loss. They turned toward the noise.

Rosemary was standing in front of the fridge holding a pitcher of orange juice, donning a Cheshire cat grin. "Good morning," she recited in a sugary tone.

Bella's entire demeanor changed. She stepped out of Lucas' hold and rubbed her clothes roughly as if she were trying to wipe him away. Lucas turned back to Rosemary. If his eyes were bullets, she'd be fucking dead.

"You're outta here," Lucas informed.

"Don't be silly," Rosemary chucked. "You know I have nowhere else to go."

"I don't care," Lucas barked.

"She's right. Besides, I need her to stay close. She's the only witness I have."

Lucas growled and left the kitchen. He needed desperately to adjust his cock, which was stretching the fuck out of his slacks. He would have his time with Bella. And the next time, there would be no interruptions.

CHAPTER ELEVEN

TAYLOR

Taylor sat patiently in the outer office of the commander. She had been medically deemed fit for duty, and it was to be her first day back on the job. She hadn't so much as stepped foot into a police station since she'd been shot, but she felt as though she was physically and mentally prepared to hit the streets. But, as soon as Taylor did step one foot into the station, she was summoned to the commander's office. And, there, she'd been waiting for thirty-five minutes.

Taylor was in the latter stages of boredom as she sat in the hard chair and peeled the nail polish from her nail, when, mercifully, the commander poked his head out of his office and told her that she could enter.

Taylor hopped out of her seat and entered the commander's office. She wouldn't sit unless instructed, so she stood in front of his desk. The commander smiled and held his hand out toward the chair facing his desk, gesturing for her to sit.

CREED 2
by *Phoenix Daniels*

"Please, accept my apology for making you wait so long. I was on the phone with headquarters trying to figure out what to do with you."

Taylor was confused. "What to do with me?" she asked.

"Please, Officer Montgomery, have a seat."

Taylor sat and waited for him to explain. Commander Evans was a newly-promoted commander. So, she'd never met him before. However, she had heard good things about him. He was said to be tough but fair. She'd heard that he was a good cop back in his day and a good supervisor. He'd moved up the ranks pretty fast based on his work ethic alone. And, in his late thirties or maybe early forties, he was pretty young to be such a high-ranking boss.

"Well, Officer Montgomery, you do realize that we can't put you back on the street, right?"

"No, sir. I hadn't realized that at all. Why not?"

"Realistically, putting you back on the street would be a disaster."

Taylor inhaled a deep breath but said nothing. She would wait for him to explain because she wasn't about to ask him why again."

"You see, Officer, from what I hear, you're engaged to the governor of Illinois. You've already had some run-ins with the press, and the powers that be fear that the media would prohibit you and your fellow officers from doing your jobs without distraction."

Taylor was no idiot. She knew that the press would be an issue. She just figured that they'd be done with her whenever the next good story came along.

"Putting you back on the street would be a public relations nightmare. The press would be all over you. Imagine everything you do and say being caught on camera."

Shit, he had a point. Taylor wasn't exactly the warm and fuzzy police.

"Okay, so, what did headquarters decide to do with me?"

"They told me to figure it out," Commander Evans said with a chuckle. "They really have no clue what to do with you."

Wow!

One would think that she was a leper.

"So, here's the thing, Officer. Since I'm newly-appointed, I don't have a secretary. I'm offering you the job. Whaddaya say?"

CREED 2
by *Phoenix Daniels*

Taylor leaned back in her chair. Although the secretary to the commander was a coveted position for some, Taylor hadn't joined the police department to be a secretary. But, alas, she ultimately had no other choice. It was either that or working in call back, doing police reports over the phone.

"I say I'll take it. Thank you, sir."

"Very well," the commander said with a smile. He stood and held his hand out.

Taylor stood and placed her hand in his.

"It'll work out well for both of us," he said as they shook.

Taylor smiled and hoped that it would.

*****

Taylor was setting the table for dinner just as Victor and Gregor entered the front door.

"Miss Montgomery," Gregor greeted before proceeding down the hall.

"Hello, Gregor. I already swept the house!" she shouted at his back.

CREED 2
by *Phoenix Daniels*

It was no use. Taylor knew that he wasn't listening. Ever since Collier's betrayal, Gregor trusted no one. He always checked for himself, taking no one's word for anything.

Victor smiled, revealing those sexy dimples, and walked over to Taylor.

"Is he ever going to call me *Taylor*?"

"Probably not." Victor chuckled.

He grabbed Taylor by the waist and pulled her against his hard body. He lowered his mouth to hers and kissed her like he missed her. Taylor snaked her arms around his neck and held him tight as he greeted her the way she loved him to. Taylor expressed her pleasure with a moan. Victor tasted of mint and promise as he kissed her angst away.

Taylor groaned her disappointment when he eased his lips from hers. He looked down at her with a smile in his eyes. Taylor gazed up into his dazzling greens.

"Hey, baby," she said softly.

"Hey, sweetness. I want to hear all about your first day back to work. But, first, I wanna get out of this suit."

Reluctantly, Taylor released him when he took a step back. He ran his fingers through her thick, curly afro and kissed her forehead.

by *Phoenix Daniels*

"I love your hair like this."

The smooth, rumble of his deep voice sent chills down Taylor's spine. "I know you do, bae."

Victor smiled and gripped Taylor's ass. "What's for dinner? Did you cook?"

"I did," Taylor said with a wide smile. "I made Beef Wellington."

Victor stepped back and did a sexy Magic Mike roll while stripping teasingly out of his suit coat. "Awe, shit, girl! You cooked white people food for your man," he chortled, playfully.

Taylor cracked up at his silliness. But he was right. She'd often teased him that Beef Wellington was rich, white people's food. But it was his favorite, so she had perfected the recipe.

"You're so silly, bae. Go on and get comfortable," she ordered through laughter.

Gregor glared curiously as Victor danced past him. He turned to Taylor with a questioning glare.

"He's nuts." Taylor chuckled. "You gonna come inside for dinner?"

"I can't. I need to secure the perimeter."

Taylor crossed her arms and glared at him. "Gregor, you ain't a one-man security force. There's a whole team out there. Now, come on and sit down." Taylor could tell that he was engaged in an inner debate. "I insist," she told him before the side that wanted to stand guard outside could win the debate.

"Alright, ma'am. Thank you," he acquiesced.

Gregor removed his jacket and walked over to the sink to wash his hands. "May I help with something?" he asked.

"Yep. Grab a bottle of Pinot Noir from the rack. There's a corkscrew in that drawer," Taylors said, pointing to the drawer under the wine rack.

"Got it."

"So, Gregor, since you're being so compliant, do you think that you could call me *Taylor*?"

"Don't push it, Miss Lady," Gregor snickered with a raised eyebrow.

Taylor laughed and finished setting the table.

"I see she bullied you into staying for dinner," Victor joked when he returned to the dining room.

Taylor laughed again, but the sight of Victor in a white, V-neck tee and gray jogging pants stole her laughter. Even dressed down, he was a vision of power and masculinity. His bulky shoulders and muscular chest formed the sexiest of silhouette under a plain, white T-shirt. And the gray jogging pants couldn't even begin to hide his powerful thighs and that massive tool between them.

"Stop staring at me like that. I'm not a piece of meat," Victor smirked.

Taylor knew that she was staring, but it wasn't a person in the room that could make her stop. Victor was mistaken. He *was* meat, pure beefcake. And she was still gaping at his noticeable bulge when Gregor placed the bottle of wine on the table louder than he needed to. Taylor quickly turned to Gregor with an apologetic grin.

"My bad," she mumbled. "You guys sit. I'll get the food."

Taylor hurried into the kitchen and grabbed a set of potholders. She pulled the hot casserole dish from the oven and carried it into the dining room.

"Mmm, Taylor, sweetheart, that smells delicious," Victor praised.

"It does," Gregor agreed.

"Thank you. I hope you like it."

CREED 2
by *Phoenix Daniels*

Taylor returned to the kitchen and grabbed two dishes. One containing potatoes au gratin and the other filled with steamed asparagus. She carried them into the dining room and placed them on mats next to the main dish.

"Baby, you have outdone yourself today. Dinner looks amazing. Sit down. I'll pour the wine."

Victor stood and grabbed the bottle of wine and poured Taylor a full glass. He attempted to pour some for Gregor, but he covered the rim.

"I'm on duty, sir."

"Nonsense, we're enjoying dinner. I'm insisting that you take the night off. Now, move your hand."

"Um-mm," Gregor refused, shaking his head. "Don't like wine, sir."

Gregor turned to Taylor. "Got any beer?" he asked.

"Of course." Taylor chuckled. "Miller Lite okay?"

"Perfect."

Taylor stood from her chair, but Victor stilled her by holding out his hand.

"Relax, babe. I'll get the beer."

Taylor lowered herself to sit. When Victor left the room, she looked over at Gregor. She could tell that he was a bit uncomfortable with Victor serving him. "Shi-id, Gregor. You're off duty. Enjoy it while you can," she urged.

"Yeah," Gregor muttered. "You keep cooking like this, and maybe I'll be able to get him to wash my car."

"Don't count on that." Taylor giggled.

When Victor returned with Gregor's beer, the three of them sat and feasted on dinner over light conversation. Taylor had to admit that she was enjoying Gregor's company. He'd opened up about his personal life for the first time since she'd met him. He was usually all about the business of keeping Victor safe.

During dinner, Taylor learned that Gregor used to be a Navy Seal, and he was a divorced father of two teenage boys that almost matched him in height. As they shared a meal, Taylor discovered that the normally brooding and intimidating giant was actually funny and charismatic. To Taylor's surprise, Gregor had opened up about everything from his political views to his parenting style. After dinner, Taylor felt as if she knew him so much better. When he was protecting Victor, he seemed almost robotic. But, now, Taylor understood that even though he took his job seriously, he was still a human being. He'd even stuck around for an after-dinner drink.

CREED 2
by *Phoenix Daniels*

"Alright, now. I gotta get home and make sure the girls that my sons sneaked in the house don't get pregnant," Gregor announced.

Taylor laughed hysterically. The effects of the wine and the fact that Gregor actually had a sense of humor gave her the giggles.

"Alright, old man, I'll see you in the morning." Victor chuckled.

As Victor walked Gregor to the door, Taylor cleared the dishes. She was bent over, placing them in the dishwasher when Victor walked up behind her and pressed his dick against her behind. He groped her ass and moaned.

"Baby, you got the sweetest ass I've ever seen."

Taylor stood upright and turned to face him. "You think so?" she asked flirtatiously.

"Most definitely. Come here," he demanded, pulling her into his arms and gripped her ass.

"Dinner was amazing," he praised as he pulled her yoga pants off of her ass.

Victor slid her pants, along with her panties, down her thighs, until they fell to the floor. He helped Taylor step out of her pants, one leg at a time. Taylor's nipples hardened and her pussy throbbed with anticipation.

Victor looked up at her and graced her with his sexiest smirk. "I repeat, dinner was amazing. But there's only one problem."

"What's that?" Taylor whispered.

"I'm still hungry," he revealed with a sexy pout.

Victor ran a single finger up her leg and then up the inside of her thigh, ultimately reaching the eager V that would lead to her pleasure. Taylor relaxed, placing her elbows on the countertop. At Victor's insistence, she eased her legs apart.

Taylor inhaled a sharp breath when Victor's thumb pressed her swollen clit. He circled the burning bundle of nerves just slow enough to inflict the sweetest torture. Taylor's breathing increased and her heart began to race. Her legs began to quiver, and she was ready to beg for relief. Seemingly, sensing her need, Victor placed his warm mouth against her quivering, wet pussy and sucked her clit into his mouth.

"Damn, Victor!" Taylor blurted breathlessly.

Her outburst must have served as the incantation used to evoke the pussy-eating beast that resided in Victor Creed. With unrelenting fierceness, he licked and sucked Taylor's pussy until she cried out in ecstasy. She reached down, clawed his scalp, and rolled her hips until she was fucking his face. Taylor was pulling his face so deep into her pussy until she was worried that he couldn't breathe. But his own pleasurable moans convinced her that he was getting the air that he needed.

Taylor rolled her shoulders back and used her free hand to fondle her sensitive nipple. The sheer pleasure of it all was almost too much. But it was when Victor slipped his thick middle finger in her wet entrance that she really lost control. Victor was licking, sucking, and finger fucking her pussy into submission, and Taylor was cumming.

"Aghh!"

Her orgasm rolled over her like a tsunami. Out of breath, quivering, and no longer able to stand on her own, Taylor's knees buckled. Although Victor caught her in his arms, he had no intention of cuddling. He flipped her around and bent her over the kitchen sink. Victor smacked her ass, grabbed the back of her neck, and pushed her head down. Taylor held on tight as Victor guided his thick dick inside her pussy. She held her breath until she adjusted to his size.

Though he was merciful with his initial invasion, all compassion flew out of the window when he retracted his dick and then returned it with a powerful thrust. He repeated the forceful act, completely lifting Taylor from her feet.

"Goddamn it, Taylor! This pussy is so wet, baby," Victor growled. "My sweet pussy!"

"Y-yesss," Taylor struggled.

Victor was filling every inch of her as if he'd literally stepped inside of her body. He grunted and groaned as he fucked her off her feet.

Taylor was gripping the faucet so tight, she was surprised that it was still attached. Each powerful thrust was all the way in, and all the way out. He was fucking Taylor into a frenzy. With his balls slapping and teasing her clit with each stroke, Taylor was peeking another explosion.

"I'm gonna cum, baby," Taylor panted.

"Cum, bae! I'm cummin' with you!"

Victor's strokes intensified as he plunged in and pulled out of her heat. Taylor's soaked pussy was pulsating on his overly generous, rock-hard dick as she erupted around him.

"I'm cumming!" Victor growled.

Taylor's toes curled as he pumped his hot seed into her. She released the faucet and gripped the edge of the sink. She was holding on tight, trying to calm her quivering legs as Victor eased his dick past her swollen, tender lower lips.

"Damn, babe," Victor mumbled out of breath. He helped Taylor to her feet and pulled her back to his chest. Victor hugged her tightly around the waist and kissed the side of her face.

"I love you so much," he rasped.

"I love you too, baby," Taylor purred.

"Leave the dishes. Let's go to bed. I'm ready for dessert."

Before she could agree or disagree, Victor swung her around, lifted her into his arms, and carried her to the bedroom.

CHAPTER TWELVE

BELLA

Bella walked into her living room and tossed her keys on the table by the door. She dropped her bag on the floor and flipped the light switch on. As she walked down the hall to her bedroom, she noticed that the bathroom light was on. Dean must've been there. She stopped at the bathroom and peered inside. Dean had his head under the cabinet. Bella smiled, happy that he was installing her brand-new basin. Bella leaned against the doorframe. After a long day of searching with no possible leads on who her mystery woman was, Dean had just made her day.

"You have got to be the best ex-husband ever," Bella admitted.

"Yeah, I'll bet," Dean scoffed. "How was your day?"

Bella blew out an exasperated breath. "Don't ask," she warned. "How bout you? How was work?"

"My client is guilty as fuck." Dean chuckled.

Dean was a criminal defense attorney, and he believed passionately that everyone deserved a proper defense. But he hated defending clients he knew were guilty. Nevertheless, he did his best to give all of his clients the best defense possible.

"You sure?" Bella asked.

"Yep. What's up with your black widow?"

Bella rubbed her temple, exhaled a frustrated breath, and ran her fingers roughly through her hair. "That bitch is invisible."

"Nobody's invisible. You'll get ya girl."

"Yeah, but in the meantime, I need you."

Dean slid from under the sink and looked up at Bella.

"What do you need exactly?"

"I need a date for Taylor's birthday party tomorrow."

Dean placed his back against the cabinet and raised a brow at Bella. "I'm not about to be your beard, Bella."

"I don't think that's what that means," Bella scoffed.

"Whatever. I'm not about to help you avoid dude. You obviously got a thing for him. Why do you keep runnin' from that man?"

"I don't have a thing for him. Not really. He's just…well, he's just real sexy. But I don't want to get involved."

"Why? Because he's *white*?"

CREED 2
by *Phoenix Daniels*

Bella huffed and rolled her eyes. "Why does everybody keep asking me that like I'm some kind of racist?" Bella asked, exasperated.

"Bella, I know you better than you know yourself. You don't want to get caught up with dude because you're afraid that your parents won't approve."

Bella opened her mouth, ready to argue, but she thought better of it. Dean was right about one thing. Bella could never bring a white man home to meet her folks. Her mother was Native American for goodness sakes. White people had practically annihilated her entire race. And not to mention the fact that her dad was black. That was a can of worms that Bella wouldn't dare open in front of her parents. But that didn't stop Bella from thinking of Lucas every free moment of her day.

It had been three weeks since Lucas Creed had rendered her a breathless, horny fool in his kitchen. Bella's traitorous body just wouldn't let her forget the man.

Dean stood to his feet and walked over to Bella. He pulled her closed and hugged her tight. "Bella, your parents have found the great loves of their lives in each other. You gotta worry about finding the great love of *your* life."

Bella slapped Dean on the back and pushed out of his grasp. "Yeah, yeah, yeah. Will you come with me or not?"

"Nope," Dean replied simply. He kissed her forehead and returned to the bathroom floor. He tucked his head under the sink and resumed the task of installing Bella's sink.

"I take it back," Bella huffed. "You're a sucky ex-husband!"

"Yep. I know," Dean muttered. "Gone and get outta here. I'm busy."

"Fuuuck you!" Bella cursed.

"See? You need a dick in that nasty mouth of yours. Stop trying to play hard to get."

Bella rolled her eyes and walked to her bedroom. She plopped down on the bed and pulled her phone out of her bra. She was tempted to call Taylor and tell her that she wasn't gonna make her birthday party. Truthfully, she was avoiding Lucas. But it wasn't for the reason that everyone assumed.

Yes, her parents more than likely would have a problem with her dating a white man, but Bella had defied her parents on many occasions. The truth was Bella was afraid. She'd only been in love once in her life, and the love of her life had turned out to be gay. Bella didn't feel as if she were strong enough to endure another painfully failed love affair.

"Every man ain't me, Belladonna Devereaux!" Dean shouted from the bathroom as if he had read her mind.

Bella ignored Dean's last comment. She got up and walked into the master bathroom to run herself a bath. That's exactly what she needed. A nice hot bath followed by a good night's sleep.

With or without Dean, she had to make an appearance at her friend's birthday party. Taylor had had a rough year, and she deserved a celebration.

Bella sighed and walked over to her dresser. She grabbed her old LSU T-shirt and an unattractive, yet comfortable, pair of panties. She returned to the bathroom and tossed her bed clothes on the vanity. As she stripped out of her work attire, she glanced at her form in the mirror. Dean had told her a million times that she was beautiful and that his sexual preference had nothing to do with her. Nevertheless, since he came out, Bella's self-esteem had taken a huge hit.

Bella slipped the ponytail holder off of her wrist and pulled her hair into a tight bun. She turned from the mirror and walked over to the tub. She carefully dipped her toe to check the

by *Phoenix Daniels*

water temperature. It was perfect. She stepped in and ease her butt into the water. Once she adjusted to the heat, Bella submerged herself in the hot water and relaxed against the back of the tub. She sighed, closed her eyes, and allowed the water to wash away her stress. But, to Bella's dismay, the second she closed her eyes, Lucas Creed's handsome face and gorgeous green eyes appeared. His full, soft lips were taunting her. Memories of the way he'd kissed her caused her entire body to tingle and stiffen. Her stomach was in knots, and she could feel tightening in her core.

Bella forced her eyes open and grabbed the body wash from the corner of the tub. She was gonna wash her ass and get the hell out of the tub. It was bad enough that the man was stalking her dreams. Bella wasn't about to let him haunt her while she was wide awake.

As if she actually had a choice.

CHAPTER THIRTEEN

BLACK WIDOW

She was sitting across the street from Arcadia, watching expensive limousines, Town Cars, and SUV's arrive one by one. She was definitely in the right place. The client's intel was on point. Because the only way a billionaire, a senator, the lieutenant governor, and the mayor would show up for some beat cop's birthday party was if she was fucking the governor. The guest list was indeed impressive, but the most shocking of arrivals was that of Luca and Francis Savelli.

What the hell were the Sicilians doing at this chick's party? Their presence could be problematic. Both men arrived heavily guarded. And, surprisingly, both had a black woman on their arm. Hell, if Sloane knew that either one of them was down with the swirl, she would have thrown her horse in that race a long time ago. Well, it wasn't too late. Sloane hadn't met a man that she couldn't have. Once she finished the job that she'd been paid to do, she would seriously consider arranging a couple of *chance* meetings with Francis Savelli. There was an air of power that swarmed around him. He was irresistibly handsome, and Lord, could he fill out a suit. Francis was definitely Sloane's type.

Sloane Vidal was the product of a black pimp and a French whore. But it didn't go in the order that most expected. Her black mother, Aubree Le Gall, was one of Cannes most notorious souteneurs. Without discrimination, she sold men, women, and children. Sadly, she wasn't even above selling her own daughter. But Sloane didn't have time to shed a tear for her horrible childhood. She had a job to do, and failure was not an option. She'd never missed a target and she wasn't about to start with Rosemary Creed.

After an hour of watching the entrance, Sloane came to the conclusion that her target was going to be a no-show. So, she'd have to use the same method of interrogation on the governor's girl that she had used on the driver and the press secretary.

Rosemary had eluded her in Louisiana, but a source revealed that she could be found in Chicago. Sloane would bet money that she ran straight to her heavily guarded husband. Getting to the governor's wife wasn't going to be easy, but Sloane had five million reasons to get the job done. She flipped the visor and checked her lipstick in the mirror. She blew herself a quick kiss, hopped out of the car, and headed toward the fancy restaurant.

CHAPTER FOURTEEN

TAYLOR

Taylor smiled because of the way Victor looked at her. No matter what, he always made her feel beautiful. It was way beyond telling her how special he thought she was. Every time he looked at her, he expressed an appreciation and a longing for her. To Taylor, it was like no other feeling in the world. No man had ever come even close to making her as happy as Victor did.

If she were smart, Taylor would have kept her eyes on her beautiful man, but she ruined the moment by looking behind him.

"Ugh!" Taylor grunted.

Victor frowned curiously. "What is it, babe?" he asked.

"Ruth Buchanan," Taylor muttered under her breath.

Victor chuckled and kissed Taylor's forehead. "Behave," he warned playfully.

Taylor would behave. After all, Carl and Ruth Buchanan were invited guests; Invited by Victor, but invited none the less.

"Smile, sweetheart," Victor whispered as he turned in the lieutenant governor's direction.

CREED 2
by *Phoenix Daniels*

For Victor, Taylor would play the game. She did her very best to make her smile appear sincere. And it was hard. She couldn't stand Ruth. The woman was a snob, and Taylor would bet a finger that she was racist as well. When Victor first introduced Taylor to lieutenant governor and his wife, Ruth's greeting was less than enthusiastic. It was as if she'd been forced to say hello against her will. Since that moment, it was Taylor who had to be forced against her will to speak.

"Taylor, you're as beautiful as ever," Carl greeted with a smile.

Taylor held her hand out to shake his hand, but instead of shaking it, Carl placed her hand to his lips. The look of disgust on Ruth's pasty face was almost worth the wet spot that he had left on her hand.

"Thank you, Carl. It's nice to see you. I'm glad you could make it," Taylor replied, wiping her hand on Victor's pants leg.

She would smile and be polite, but she had no absolutely no intention of being the first to speak. His stank-ass wife would have to humble herself enough to greet the *little people.*

For seconds, there was an awkward silence. Victor and Carl seemed to notice that neither woman was going to speak.

Victor placed his hand in the small of Taylor's back and chuckled softly. Admittedly, Taylor was proud when Victor didn't try to fill the silence by speaking to Ruth. No matter what, the man had her back.

Carl cleared his throat nervously and asked. "Well, are you ready for Monday's press conference?"

"Hmm, let's see. Am I ready to be crucified for trying to fix the state's budget deficit by placing a bullshit tax on shit that people are addicted to? Yeah, sure, I'm stoked," Victor scoffed.

"What lies are you gentlemen over here telling in this corner?"

The voice came from behind. Ruth's dead eyes awakened instantly. As a matter of fact, they even sparkled a bit. Taylor turned, sure that she already knew who was putting a rose to Ruth's saggy cheeks. It was Jack Storm, of course. His good looks could wake the dead. Hence, Ruth Buchanan.

"Jack Storm," Victor greeted with a smile. "How the hell are you?"

The two shook hands.

"I can't complain. Taylor, you look amazing. I see that you're still slummin' with politicians."

CREED 2
by *Phoenix Daniels*

"Says the slimy one percenter," Victor scoffed.

Jack released a hearty laugh and rebutted with, "I see you managed to squeeze your way into the percentile."

"Lies!" Victor blurted. "Jack, you know Carl and Ruth, don't you?"

"I do. Carl, Ruth, hello."

Before Carl could return the salutation, Ruth stepped forward with a big smile and placed her hand on Jack's arm. "Jack, it is so good to see you again," Ruth crooned.

She was rubbing Jack's arm as if he belonged to her. Taylor couldn't believe Ruth's inappropriate behavior, and right in front of her husband. Carl's face turned beet red with embarrassment.

Jack's smile fell. He looked down at Ruth's hand on his arm and frowned. At that very moment, Taylor wished that she was a mind reader. But, in true Jack Storm fashion, she didn't need the special power. Because Jack never held back.

"Why, Ruth? Why is it so good to see me? Do I owe you money?"

Taylor fought back a giggle. The woman couldn't so much as say hello to her, but she was all over Jack.

CREED 2
by *Phoenix Daniels*

Ruth laughed nervously, but she didn't remove her hand from Jack's arm. Unfortunately for Ruth, Jack's wife, Victoria Storm, walked up. The look on her face expressed that she would be very happy to remove the woman's hand from her husband.

"Hello, Victoria," Ruth greeted in weirdly high pitch.

"Ruth, take your hand off my husband," Victoria uttered without even looking in her direction.

Even though her tone lacked any emotion, Ruth somehow knew that she meant business. Obviously, embarrassed, Ruth slid her hand off of Jack's arm and moved closer to her husband.

"Hello, Carl," Victoria greeted.

"Mrs. Storm," the lieutenant governor returned.

It was funny to see how people behaved around the Storms. They were Victor's largest contributors, and the Buchanan's acted accordingly. Little did they know that Jack wasn't the type of person to hold his money over their heads. But Victor wasn't about to tell them that. He'd once mentioned to Taylor that he enjoyed watching Carl and his wife squirm in Jack's presence.

Victoria turned to Taylor with open arms. "Happy birthday, baybee!" she squealed as she pulled Taylor into a hug.

"Thanks, Vic," Taylor grunted through the bear hug.

Victoria stepped back and turned to Victor. "Ello, guvnah," she said in a really bad British accent.

"Victoria," Victor returned, "As lovely as ever, you are."

"Well, thank you, Victor. You ain't too bad on the eyes yourself," Victoria replied with a wink.

"Stop flirting before you get a spanking," Jack threatened.

Victoria laughed. She waved off Jack's fake jealousy and grabbed Taylor's hand. "Will you gentlemen, please excuse us? I need to borrow the birthday girl for a minute."

Victor nodded and lifted his glass to those sexy lips. Taylor suddenly couldn't wait for her birthday party to be over so she could spend some naked time with her man. However, that would have to wait, she thought, as Victoria led her away.

"Stay out of trouble!" Jack shouted at their backs.

Victoria giggled but kept walking.

"Where are we going?" Taylor asked.

"To our table. I've assembled the girls to talk about our spa day."

"Spa day?"

"Yes, tomorrow. It's been a trying year for all of us, and we need to de-stress. So, we're gonna get pampered. I'm treating you and your friends."

"Oh, shit, Vic. That is so sweet. My friends, huh?"

Victoria turned to Taylor with narrowed eyes. "*Most* of your friends," Victoria corrected.

"Nope. Too late. You said *my friends*."

Victoria rolled her eyes.

"Vic, neither you nor Bella ever told me why you don't get along. What happened between you two?"

Victoria's steps halted. She turned to Taylor. She was seemingly having a debate within about whether or not to share her business with Taylor. "Donatella," Victoria said softly.

"Donatella? Bella's sister? What about her?"

"We had a thing," Victoria shrugged.

"Whaaaat?" Taylor exclaimed. "You and Donna?"

"Keep your voice down," Victoria blurted in a hushed tone. "Yes. We were together for a few months."

Taylor was stunned. She knew that Victoria went both ways, but she'd had no idea that Donatella was into women too.

"What happened? And what does that have to do with you and Bella?" Taylor asked.

"Well, long story short, I told Donna from the very beginning that I wasn't looking for anything serious, but she got in her feelings. When she started getting possessive, I broke it off."

Taylor frowned. "You broke her heart," she whispered.

It was Victoria's turn to frown. "Tay, she knew from the get-go that women were only a *thing* for me and that if I were to settle down, it would be with a man. She *knew* that. And besides, she ain't gay either. She's bisexual too. And she told me she wanted the same thing. But, then, she changed the game on me. So, I told her that we couldn't see each other anymore. From what I heard, Bella blames me, saying that I'm the reason that Donna transferred to narcotics and why she stays away for so long."

"So, Bella hates you because you broke her sister's heart? But why do you hate Bella?"

"She tried to come at me in the bathroom at work."

Taylor recoiled in shock. She couldn't believe what Victoria was telling her. "At work?" Taylor gasped.

"Yep."

Taylor shook her head. This shit was unreal. Neither one of them ever so much as mentioned anything about a fist fight.

"Damn. With the two of you being black belts, I'll bet that would have been one hell of a fight," Taylor mused.

"It ended before it started. Lieutenant Barnes came in."

"Oh, my God, Vic. Why didn't you tell me?"

"Why would I go around telling folks that? Besides, Donatella and I were so long ago. Why did she wait so long to say something?"

Victoria started to walk on, but Taylor grabbed her by the wrist. "Vic, you've moved on. Donna has moved on. She's been with her man for four years now. So, why can't you and Bella move on?"

Victoria's eyes widened as if she couldn't believe what just came out of Taylor's mouth.

"Because she came at me at *my job*!" Victoria spat. "She's lucky she was able to walk out of that bathroom on her own. Look, Tay, Donatella is a grown-ass woman, and she made a grown-ass decision to get involved with me. Bella didn't have shit to do with what went on between her sister and me. Besides, Donna had been trying to get into narcotics long before she started fucking with me."

"That's exactly why you don't shit where you eat," Taylor reprimanded.

"I know that now, Taylor," Victoria huffed.

Taylor sighed and released Victoria's wrist. It was clear that there wasn't going to be a resolution to the dissonance between Victoria and Bella. And, as long as they weren't throwing blows, Taylor wasn't gonna get involved. But, Bella was her friend, and Victoria was her friend too. So, they would have to learn to coexist. Taylor definitely wasn't looking forward to telling either of them that they were both bridesmaids in her wedding.

That is as soon as Victor divorced his legally dead wife.

Taylor would hold on to that little piece of disastrous information for as long as she could. Victoria continued on to her table and Taylor followed.

"She's coming to the spa day," Taylor muttered at Victoria's back.

"Whatever," Victoria grumbled without looking back. "Come on here, girl. We got plans to make."

CREED 2
by *Phoenix Daniels*

As instructed, Taylor followed Victoria to the table. Most of the ladies had already assembled. All, except Bella. She'd called Taylor earlier and told her that she would be arriving late. Bella was up to her eyeballs in murders. So, Taylor would be happy if she were able to make it at all.

"Hey, birthday girl! Great party!" Nicole shouted.

Taylor smiled at her big sister. She was clearly drunk. And Taylor wasn't mad because Nicole was the worst of control freaks. Everything with her was about decorum, and Taylor was happy to see her finally let down her hair.

Taylor walked over to her big sister and hugged her. "Are you having fun?" Taylor whispered.

"A ball!" Nicole shrieked.

"Where's Jeffrey?"

"Girl, I don't know" Nicole responded with a giggle. "I wasn't lookin' for his ass. *You* lookin' for his ass?"

Jeffrey Morgan, the water commissioner, was Nicole's fiancé. He was an overly ambitious politician and definitely not Taylor's favorite person. To Taylor, he lacked sincerity. There was no smoking gun, but something told her that his intentions where her sister was concerned weren't the best. But, for now,

CREED 2
by *Phoenix Daniels*

Taylor would have to rely on him to ensure that her intoxicated sibling got home safely.

"Jeffrey… humph!" Nicole scoffed.

Taylor squinted, studying her sister. She didn't seem right. There was something about her behavior. Something much more than just simply being drunk.

"You okay, Nic?"

"I'm goooood," Nicole sang. "I'm having a ball."

Taylor looked around the room for Jeffrey, but she didn't see him. "Well, don't forget that your mother and father are here. So, don't have too much fun."

"Yeah, yeah, yeah. I'll be good," Nicole assured.

Taylor kissed her sister's cheek and sat her down in a chair next to hers.

"She ain't feeling no pain," Maria chimed.

Maria Mendez was Taylor's partner before Taylor got benched.

"I know right." Taylor giggled under her breath.

"You ready for some fireworks?" Maria asked.

"Huh? What do you mean?"

"Look," Maria prompted, pointing her chin somewhere behind Taylor.

CREED 2
by *Phoenix Daniels*

Taylor turned to see what Maria was referencing.

Fireworks indeed.

Bella entered the restaurant on Dean's arm. Maria, along with the entire world knew that Bella and Victoria didn't get along, but what she didn't know was that there was a shitload of sexual tension between Bella and Victor's little brother, Lucas, who was now blocking Bella and Dean's path. Taylor stood to get a better view.

Lucas was donning a scowl, and Dean a smirk. Taylor laughed a bit on the inside when Dean kissed Bella's forehead and walked in the direction of the men's room, leaving her alone with Lucas. It was clear that Bella's plan to discourage Lucas' advances hadn't worked when Lucas grabbed Bella's face and ran his thumb across her cheek.

Taylor could have enjoyed watching her friend squirm a little longer, but the presence of a woman standing, just a few feet away, diverted her attention. She was tall, pretty, and well-dressed. But, for some reason, she seemed to be captivated by Taylor and her small group of friends.

Taylor smiled at the woman and looked around to see who she was with. She appeared to be alone. Taylor's intention was to walk over and engage the stranger in conversation, but the woman smiled and walked away before Taylor could make her way over to her.

Taylor shrugged it off and turned back to Bella and Lucas, but they were gone too. She said a tiny prayer that Bella would finally let down her guard and allowed herself a little fun. She had a feeling that Lucas Creed could offer her the excitement and passion that she believed her friend so desperately needed.

Taylor thought about all the shit that she was dealing with and decided that she couldn't fix the world. So, she returned to her seat next to Nicole. Maria and Victoria sat as well. Without waiting for Bella, Victoria began to lay out the details of their spa day.

CHAPTER FIFTEEN

BELLA

"Son of a bitch," Bella gritted at her disloyal ex-husband.

Dean chuckled and had the audacity to kiss her on the damn forehead. Bella had asked his ass for one thing, and that was to run interference between her and Lucas. But he couldn't even do that. When Lucas cut them off at the path, Dean politely introduced himself as a friend of the family. Then, he actually had the nerve to tell Lucas that he'd heard wonderful things about him before excusing himself to the men's room.

Reluctantly, Bella looked up at Lucas. No matter how sexy, the smirk on his handsome face was irritating.

"What?" Bella scoffed.

"Did you bring a bodyguard?"

Bella rolled her eyes. "I don't need no bodyguard for you, Lucas."

"Ha! You sure?" Lucas asked through a chuckle.

Bella opened her mouth to speak, but Lucas moved fast, closing the small distance between them. He was as close as he could be without actually touching Bella. She inhaled a sharp breath. Her heart was racing. It was her body's normal reaction to his nearness. Bella couldn't deny how her body responded when Lucas was close. He covered her face with his hands and ran his thumb across her cheek.

"I am going kiss you again, Bella," Lucas rasped passionately. "Tonight," he declared.

Bella was speechless. If there was a fight in her, it wasn't coming out. Lucas was, for lack of a better word, *compelling.*

It didn't help that Bella was running on fumes. She was working multiple homicides. And not just your everyday, run-of-the-mill homicides. The murders that she was investigating were hitting very close to home. Her friend had already been gunned down. And it was highly probable that she was still in danger.

Bella had been working overtime to find her mystery woman and bring her to justice. And, luckily, the lab was able to pull a partial print from a box of gloves that were dropped in Collier's hospital room. Although the print wasn't a match for anyone who was working in the hospital the night he was killed, it was still a long shot. The print could have belonged to anyone, from the manufacturers to distributors. What Bella needed to go forward was a positive match.

"Bella?"

Bella blinked out of her work haze and focused on Lucas' hypnotic green eyes. "Huh? What?"

"Are you okay? Where were you?" he asked with concern etched on his face.

"Oh, I'm good. Just…well, work shit," Bella admitted truthfully.

Lucas nodded as if he understood. He gripped Bella's wrist. "Come with me. Let's get you a drink."

Bella nodded. She wasn't much of a drinker, but she needed something to take the edge off. She looked back at Taylor as she allowed Lucas to lead her to the bar. Bella's eyes rolled involuntarily when she saw Victoria sitting next to her. But it wasn't Victoria's presence that concerned her as much as the woman that was standing right behind Taylor. She appeared to be overly invested in Taylor, and whatever she was saying. Bella had never seen the woman before. She could have totally been a friend that Bella had never met or someone associated with Victor. But, for some reason, Bella's sixth sense told her otherwise. She tugged at Lucas until he stopped walking.

He looked back and frowned curiously. "What?"

"Do you know that woman standing behind Taylor?"

Lucas squinted until he spotted the woman that Bella was talking about. "In the black?" he asked.

"Yeah. You know her?"

"No. She doesn't look familiar. Why?"

Bella turned to look at Lucas. "Look how close she is. Does that shit look normal to you?"

Lucas pondered the question before saying, "Maybe Taylor knows her. Or maybe she's a friend of one of Taylor's friends."

Lucas' explanation made sense since they were in one of the restaurant's private dining rooms.

"Maybe," Bella contemplated. "But maybe not. Come on. Let's go see."

Lucas looked from Bella back to the woman. "Okay, let's go," he said, grabbing her hand.

For some reason, he pulled Bella behind him, as if shielding her from danger. Bella shook her head and chuckled softly. In so many ways, Lucas reminded her of his brother. There were plenty of times when she'd observed Victor's overprotective behavior toward Taylor. It was so unnecessary.

If anyone could protect themselves, it was Taylor. She was as tough as nails. But none of that mattered to her man. He hovered none the less. And his baby brother was displaying the very same characteristics.

"Lucas Creed, is it your intention to walk right past your mother without so much as a hello?"

Lucas froze. And before Bella could help it, she walked, smack into his back. She yelped as she bounced off his solid back and struggled to regain her footing. Lucas reached out and grabbed her elbow, just as a crazy handsome, more mature Lucas lookalike grabbed her other elbow.

"Bella, I'm sorry. Are you okay?" Lucas asked, looking her up and down.

"Yeah…yes." Bella chuckled. "I'm good." She looked up at the man holding her elbow and smiled. "Hello," she greeted with a grateful smile.

"Hello," he replied as he released her elbow. "You sure that you're okay?"

"Yes, sir. I'm fine. Thank you for rescuing me."

"I rescued you too," Lucas mumbled.

Bella muffled her laughter and turned to Lucas and Victor's mother. She remembered seeing her at the hospital when Taylor was shot. Lucas held his hand out toward the handsome couple.

"Bella, I'd like you to meet my parents. My dad, Victor Creed Senior, and my mom, Dr. Tabitha Creed. Mom and Dad, meet Belladonna Devereaux."

"Hello, Senator and Dr. Creed. It's nice to meet you."

"My goodness, child, you are gorgeous. And what a beautiful name," Tabitha gushed.

Had Bella been a few shades lighter, she wouldn't have been able to hide the fact that she was blushing. And, since she was named after a poison, Bella smiled at the fact that Lucas' mom referred to her name as beautiful.

"Thank you, ma'am. You're beautiful too," Bella replied honestly.

Tabitha Creed furrowed her brows as she stared at Bella. Bella smiled nervously. She was beginning to feel a bit self-conscious.

Apparently, noticing Bella's discomfort, Tabitha smiled and said, "I've seen you before. You're the detective from the hospital. If I'm not mistaken, you were in charge of the investigation into Taylor's shooting."

Bella nodded. "Yes, ma'am. I'm still investigating it."

Tabitha's frown was an indicant of her confusion. "I thought that boy was murdered in the hospital."

"Yes, ma'am he was. But now, I'm looking for the person who murdered *him*."

Tabitha pursed her lips and ran her fingers through her red hair. "Hopefully, to give 'em a medal," Tabitha scoffed.

"Not exactly." Bella chuckled.

Lucas placed his hand in the small of Bella's back. "How about we give the shop talk a rest, Mom? This *is* a party."

Victor Senior placed his arm around his wife and kissed the side of her face. "Come on, beautiful. Let me buy you a drink." His voice was deep and melodious, and judging by his wife's reaction, it'd had the desired effect.

Dr. Creed nearly swooned. Her lashes fluttered as she raised her face, allowing him access to her lips. The two kissed as if their love affair was brand new. In a way, the Creeds reminded Bella of her own parents. Their love was something that Bella was longing for when she'd married Dean. But, for her, it just wasn't meant to be."

Bella turned back to Victoria, but the woman had disappeared. "She's gone," she whispered to Lucas.

CREED 2
by *Phoenix Daniels*

Lucas and Bella scanned the room, but she'd vanished completely.

"It was probably nothing," Lucas reassured.

But Bella wasn't completely convinced that it was nothing. She'd learned a long time ago to trust her instincts, and her instincts were telling her that she needed to at least try to find out who the woman was. Later, Bella would pull the restaurant's surveillance video.

"Mom and Dad, will you excuse us?"

"Of course, sweetheart," Tabitha responded. "It was so nice to meet you, Belladonna."

"You too, Dr. Creed."

"Tabitha," the doctor insisted.

Bella nodded and went to move away, but Lucas gripped her wrist and pulled her a few feet away from his parents.

"Where do you think you're going?"

"I am going over there to say Happy Birthday to my friend."

"What about our drink?" Lucas frowned.

"Maybe later," Bella replied.

She wiggled her wrist free and stepped away. She turned and began to walk toward Taylor's table. She smiled, knowing that he was still standing in the same spot. She could feel his eyes on her, but she didn't dare look back.

"Wassup, superstar?" Taylor greeted as she stood to her feet. She pulled Bella in for a hug.

"Hey, friend," Bella responded enthusiastically. "Happy Birthday."

"Thank you." Taylor's smiled brightly.

She was clearly having a good time, and Bella was pleased. After all the shit Taylor had been through, she deserved to have a little fun.

"Ladies, y'all know Bella," Taylor proclaimed.

"Hey, Bella!" Nicole screeched.

"Hey, Nic." Bella chuckled with furrowed brows.

Nicole is slapped.

The rest of the ladies, except for Victoria Storm, greeted in unison. So, in return, Bella spoke to everyone except her. Taylor cleared her throat loudly and shifted her disappointed glare between Bella and Victoria.

"Bella," Victoria grumbled.

"Price," Bella replied, with the satisfaction of knowing that it pissed Victoria off whenever she called her by her maiden name.

CREED 2
by *Phoenix Daniels*

"My name is Storm, bi—"

"Bella, the girls are planning a spa day tomorrow for my birthday," Taylor announced, interrupting Victoria's retort.

Bella smirked and focused her attention on Taylor. She really didn't have the energy for the back and forth with Victoria. "Spa day, huh?" she asked.

"Yeah. Since tomorrow's Sunday, and most of us will be off, we're meeting up for breakfast. Then we're gonna get pampered. And, afterward, we're gonna meet at my house for drinks."

"Unfortunately, I do have to work tomorrow. But I might be able to make it to happy hour at your place."

"By the way, how is work?" Taylor inquired."

Bella knew that Taylor wanted answers, but she didn't have any answers to give. Bella blew out a frustrated breath. "Work is unfulfilling," Bella admitted somberly.

Taylor granted Bella a sympathetic smile and rubbed her upper arm. "You'll close your cases," Taylor reassured. "You're a kickass detective."

Bella rolled her eyes when Victoria fake coughed and took a sip from her glass. She looked down at Victoria and asked, "You ain't got no other friends here?"

CREED 2
by *Phoenix Daniels*

"Just you," Victoria sneered, sarcastically.

Everything in Bella wanted to slap the shit out of Victoria Storm, and if they were in different company, she probably would have. "Taylor, I gotta go holler at the restaurant manager right quick. I'll be back in a sec."

"Okay, but, don't try to sneak outta here," Taylor warned with narrowed eyes.

"I won't. Jack and I will be sure to say bye before we leave."

Taylor's eyes widened, but Victoria only laughed.

"That's funny, Bella. How's Donatella?" Victoria taunted.

Bella masked her anger with laughter and turned to Victoria. "Donna is doing well. I'll tell her you asked about her."

"You do that." Victoria sniggered.

Bella smiled, waved to the other ladies, and went to find the restaurant manager. But, on the way, she made sure to cross paths with Jack Storm. As much as she couldn't stand Victoria, she had to admit that the women got lucky in the man department. Jack Storm had it all; looks, brains, money, and swag. Admittedly, the man was the shit. He was standing next to Victor, and the two of them, together, were a sight to see. But, as fine as Jack and Victor were, there was only one man that tightened Bella's core. And he was nowhere to be found.

Bella approached the two and spoke. "Governor, Mr. Storm, how are you, gentlemen?"

"I'm good, Bella. You're looking as lovely as ever," Victor commented.

Ever the gentleman.

"Thank you, Governor. Mr. Storm, how are you?"

Bella made sure to move closer to Jack than she normally would have. She placed her hand on his solid pec and looked into his cool blue eyes. Jack looked down at Bella and smiled, showing perfect, white teeth. He covered Bella's hand with his own, but he didn't move it away.

"You trying to make my wife jealous? Did you ladies have a falling out?" Jack asked with a mischievous grin. He chuckled and shook his head. "You might wanna be careful. My wife will bed you before I will."

Bella couldn't help but laugh.

Jack Storm couldn't be used or rattled. She had to give it to him. He was a cool dude. Too bad his wife was such a bitch.

"Alright, now," Jack urged. "Take your hand off of me before my wife embarrasses us both."

Bella giggled and dropped her hand. She turned to Victor. His lips were pressed into a thin line. He was trying unsuccessfully to suppress his laughter. Victor shook his head and threw his arm over Bella's shoulder. "Are you trying to drive my baby brother insane?"

Bella wrinkled her brow. She totally hadn't expected that from Victor. "What do you mean?"

"You know what I mean. You can tell how he feels about you."

Deciding to forgo the whole act of playing dumb, Bella asked, "What does Lucas want from me, Governor?"

"I don't know exactly," Victor answered honestly. "But I'm willing to bet that it's much more than you assume."

"Humph," Bella scoffed, crossing her arms. "Your brother is used to woman chasing him."

"And?"

"And he only wants me because I ain't chasing his ass."

"*Oh*, okay. I guess that explains why he can't keep his eyes off you and why he's always asking Taylor about you. It's

not because he's really into you, it's because you don't chase
him," Victor retorted, sarcastically.

"Whatever," Bella dismissed. "You gentlemen have a
good evening."

Bella walked away in search of the restaurant manager.
As she headed to the hostess' stand, she scanned the room for
her disloyal ex-husband. He had made his way over to Taylor's
table.

"Can I help you?" the perky young hostess asked.

Bella showed the woman her shield and told her that she
needed to speak with the manager. Her expression revealed her
curiosity. Bella could tell that she wanted to know the reason
for her request, but she didn't ask. She excused herself and went
to retrieve the manager.

While she waited, Bella peeped into the private dining
room. Her eyes landed right on Lucas. He was laughing with
Jack and Victor, baring beautiful, white teeth. Bella couldn't
deny that the man was gorgeous. Actually, he was so much
more than just gorgeous. Lucas was charismatic, educated, and
he had a great sense of humor.

Over the past few months, Bella had observed how
Lucas interacted with Taylor and his other brothers. Far from

what Bella would expect from a rich, white dude. He was definitely a catch. But it had taken Bella entirely too long to get over her love for Dean, and the loss of their marriage. To her, falling in love wasn't worth the pain of losing love.

"Miss, you wanted to see me? I'm Gary, the manager."

Bella blinked out of her Lucas haze and turned to the manager. He was smiling, but she could tell that he was a tad uneasy. Bella smiled to still his anxiety.

"Yes. I'm Detective Devereaux from the Chicago Police Department. Do you have security cameras?"

"We do."

"I need the surveillance footage from this evening in and outside the restaurant."

The manager's brow wrinkled. His face was carved with curiosity. But, unlike the hostess, he did inquire. "Why do you need this footage, Detective?"

"It's part of an on-going investigation."

The manager nodded his head. "Unfortunately, we don't have cameras inside the dining room. But we do have cameras outside and in the bar. I can make you a copy of the footage that we have."

"I'd appreciate that. I'll be in the private banquet."

"No problem. I'll find you when it's done."

"Thank you, Gary."

When the manager walked away, Bella headed back to the dining room. When she entered, she noticed that most of the guests had sat down to dinner. She crossed the room to take her seat next to Dean at Taylor's table. Seated on her other side, was Taylor's mom. Martha was beautiful, and Taylor was practically her twin. Whereas Taylor, with her thick, natural curls, was more of a bohemian beauty, Martha's look was meticulously well put together. She smiled and placed her hand on Bella's shoulder.

"Bella, how are you, darling?"

Her friendly smile incited Bella to smile. "I'm doing well, Mrs. Montgomery. How are you?"

"Wonderful," she responded sweetly.

Bella enjoyed friendly conversations throughout dinner. During the course of the evening, she observed the way that Taylor and Victor interacted with each other. Even though they were dealing with the return of his wife, they seemed to be handling it very well. The Creeds and the Montgomery's appeared to get along very well. If Taylor's parents had an issue with her relationship with a white man, they didn't show it. It was the same with Victor's parents. They seemed to love Taylor, and so did his brothers.

As she often found herself doing for the most of the evening, Bella looked over at Lucas. He was staring at his phone while simultaneously having a conversation with his brother, Lincoln. Bella looked around the room at all of Victor's brothers. She grinned and shook her head. Tabitha Creed had birthed some beautiful sons. Keeping them on the right path had to have been a hell of an undertaking.

"So, that's the man that you've been running from?" Dean whispered in her ear. "Seems to me you should be running toward him."

"Mind your business, Dean," Bella warned.

"You *are* my business, Belladonna. Now, that man is beyond good-looking, he's well off, and he is really into you. I've been watching him. His eyes have followed you around this room all night."

"Leave it alone, Dean," Bella gritted.

Dean blew out a harsh breath. His frustration was evident. But Bella didn't insert herself into his romantic life, and she wasn't going to allow him to dictate hers.

CREED 2
by *Phoenix Daniels*

"He's not *me*, Bella. That man is as straight as an arrow. Trust me. I know these things."

"Gaydar," Bella scoffed.

"Hell, yeah. Trust and believe. If I thought that man had an ounce of sugar in his tank, I would be all over that."

Bella frowned at the thought. "Dean, please, shut up."

Dean chuckled and draped his arm over Bella's shoulder. He pulled her close and kissed her forehead. "I love you, girl. I just want you to be happy. You know that, right?"

Bella relaxed against him. "I know." She breathed. "And I love you too."

LUCAS

He had introduced himself as a friend of the family, but he was all over Bella. Everything in Lucas was telling him to go and yank Bella out of her seat. But, then, everyone would think that he was insane. It was becoming clear that this Dean guy was more than just a friend. Lucas could see the guy's love for Bella in his body language. He pulled his cell phone out of his Jacket pocket and text Taylor.

Who is this guy?

Lucas looked down the table. Taylor was grinning at her phone. Seconds later, Lucas' phone buzzed.

What guy? Taylor text back.

Lucas looked over at Taylor with narrowed eyes. She raised her hands, feigning ignorance as if she didn't know who in the hell Lucas was talking about.

Don't play with me, Taylor!

Okay, okay! That's Bella's ex-husband.

Ex?

Yeah.

Then, why is he here?

They're still friends.

CREED 2
by *Phoenix Daniels*

Friends? They look more than friendly.

Trust me, Lucas. They're just friends.

Lucas stuffed his phone back inside his pocket and looked over at Bella. She was leaning on her *so-called* ex as he kissed her forehead. No longer wanting to watch the show, he stood suddenly.

Lincoln looked up at him with a puzzled expression.

"What's up, bro?"

"I'm going to the bar," Lucas grunted.

"Oh, good. Bring me back a vodka and tonic."

"I looked like a fucking waiter?" Lucas snapped as he walked away.

He knew that he was taking his foul mood out on his brother, but shit, that's what brothers were for. He made his way to the bar and ordered himself a shot of Don Julio. He knocked it back and gestured for the bartender to give him another one.

Lucas wanted Bella, and he could tell that she wanted him to some degree. But, if she was in love with another man, Lucas had no intention of throwing his hat in the ring. He took the second shot and looked around the restaurant. There were

CREED 2
by Phoenix Daniels

plenty of fish in the sea. Maybe he could get drunk, find a hot woman, and fuck Bella out of his brain.

"I'll have one of those," a male behind Lucas said.

When he turned around, he was face to face with Bella's ex-husband.

"Give him another," Dean told the bartender.

Lucas stood to his full height and looked the man in his eye. He was smiling, so he didn't expect trouble. But, if there was to be trouble, Lucas was more than ready.

Getting right to the point, Dean asked, "So, you got a thing for Bella?"

"Is that a problem?"

Dean chuckled softly. "Not with me. I can see you two together."

Lucas' brows furrowed. He didn't quite understand what was happening. "Do you still love her?" he asked, pointedly.

"I do," he admitted, but he dropped his head as if he was sad.

Lucas really wanted to know the dynamic of their relationship. And, just as he was getting ready to ask, the bartender sat two shots in front of them. Dean picked up the shots and handed one to Lucas.

"Down the hatch," he toasted before taking his shot.

Lucas took his shot and slammed the glass on the bar. "So, if you still love her, how can you see us together?"

"I'm gay, Lucas. I love Bella with all my heart, but I can't deny who I am."

Lucas was stunned. He would have never guessed that Dean was gay. To be honest, he didn't fit Lucas' stereotypical idea of a gay man. He looked more like an NFL player.

"When Bella and I got married, I was totally in love with her. I dreamed of having a normal life, including a family. The only problem was there was nothing *normal* about me. I strived to be a good husband. I fought to be straight. But, in the end, I am who I am. And, after coming to that realization, I hurt Bella more than she'd ever been hurt before."

"Awe, shit, man." Lucas breathed.

The thought of the pain that Bella must've felt was distressing. It was no wonder why she was constantly running from him. She had to have major trust issues with men and relationships in general.

"Is she still in love with you?" Lucas had to ask.

"Naw. She doesn't love me in *that* way. But she is the only family that I have left. So, you should know that if you do get involved, I'm not going anywhere."

"Fair enough. But, if we *do* get together, you'll have to keep your mouth off of her."

Dean's eyes lit up with amusement. "I'll do my best." He chuckled.

"Naw, fuck your best. Keep your lips to yourself."

Dean laughed and patted Lucas on the shoulder. "Don't get ahead of yourself," he uttered. He tossed a fifty on the bar and walked away.

Lucas went back into the dining room and searched for Bella. He found her chatting it up with Taylor. Taylor was laughing, and Lucas would bet that she was ratting him out about his text messages.

He maneuvered around the tables and made his way over to the ladies. Bella smiled, and Lucas was astounded by her beauty. Bella didn't smile much. Well, not around Lucas anyway. But, when she did, she was blindingly beautiful. Her natively, reddish complexion was glowing. She had her long, black hair pulled into a high pony that hung down her back. And so tempting was her lean but femininely curvy body was in the black, strapless dress. The more he looked at her, the more he had to have her. And, before the night was over, he would.

CHAPTER SIXTEEN

TAYLOR

"I still can't believe that you brought Dean to block for you," Taylor said through laughter.

"It didn't work," Bella scoffed. "That traitor introduced himself as a friend of the family."

"Girl, you need to stop fighting it. You have been watching that man all night."

"What? Girl, please," Bella protested. "No, I wasn't."

"Lies! And what was that shit you were pulling with Jack?"

Bella laughed. "I was just fucking with your friend."

"Shi-id. You might have turned her on." Taylor giggled.

"Girl, bye." Bella sneered with a roll of her eyes.

Taylor stopped laughing as if something behind Bella had captured her attention. "Heyyy, Lucas," Taylor practically sang.

Bella reluctantly turned around. For most of the night, she'd been able to avoid his seductive glare.

"Bella, have I mentioned how beautiful you look tonight?"

160

"No, but thank you," Bella replied coolly.

Taylor could sense Bella's relief when Lucas turned his attention to her.

"Are you enjoying your birthday?"

"I am," Taylor beamed.

And she really was. Taylor loved celebrating with her friends and family. Their presence provided the greatest of distractions. She hadn't thought about Rosemary's return in hours. And, admittedly, watching Bella squirm around Lucas was strangely entertaining.

"Bella, can I have a word?" Lucas requested.

Bella nodded and smiled. But, behind her smile, Taylor saw anxiety. And she understood why. Taylor could only imagine, not only the pain of learning that her husband was gay, but it also had to be a major blow to her ego. However, she did want Bella to be happy again. She wanted Bella to face her fear and allow someone in. If not Lucas, then some other deserving man.

Lucas possessively placed his hand in the small of Bella's back. He was prepared to lead her away. But, before he could, Dean walked up and handed Bella a glass of white wine. Taylor could see Lucas' disappointment and Bella's relief.

CREED 2
by *Phoenix Daniels*

"I'm so sorry, Bella. Something has come up, and I have to go." Dean turned to Lucas, smiling conspiratorially. "Lucas, do you think you can drive Bella home for me?"

Bella's mouth flew open, but she said nothing. Taylor pressed her lips together and struggled not to laugh at her friend.

"Go, and take care of your business. It would be my pleasure to see Bella home." He turned to Bella with a smirk. "My pleasure," he mouthed.

Bella's lips quivered as if she was attempting to speak, but Dean leaned down and kissed her cheek. "I'll catch up with you later," he said before walking away, leaving Bella with her mouth open.

"Well, since we're gonna be alone in the car, I guess our talk can wait until later."

Bella's mouth was still open when Lucas strolled away. Once the coast was clear, Taylor burst into laughter.

CREED 2
by *Phoenix Daniels*

BELLA

Bella thanked the manager for the disc and crept toward the door. Her plan was to sneak out of the restaurant and walk around the corner to request an Uber. When she stepped outside, the cool night air kissed her face. Bella took a deep breath. But, before she could exhale, she heard...

"Going somewhere?"

She turned to her right to find Lucas leaning against the brick wall. "I don't wanna be a bother. I can hop in an Uber."

"It's no bother at all, Bella. I'd be happy to take you home," Lucas assured with a sexy smirk. "As a matter of fact, here we are now."

Just as Bella looked up, a valet pulled a black Land Rover to the curb.

"Shall we?" Lucas offered.

With his hand pressed to her back, he ushered her to the SUV. A surge of heat traveled throughout her entire body. Bella wouldn't dare try to deny her attraction to Lucas. In fact, she was more than attracted to him. She would even venture to say that she was captivated.

CREED 2
by Phoenix Daniels

Bella allowed him to help her inside the vehicle. She watched as he walked around the front of the SUV. Lucas walked with a self-assuredness that most didn't possess. He had more of a strut than a walk. He was extremely handsome. And, judging by the confident way he carried himself, he knew it.

Lucas climbed into the vehicle and looked over at Bella. "Seatbelt," he ordered with a smile. "It's the law."

"I know the law," Bella muttered as she fastened her seatbelt.

When Lucas turned the ignition, Guns N' Roses' "Sweet Child O' Mine" blared from the speakers. He quickly turned down the volume and apologized. Bella nodded, but she didn't mind. The song happened to be one of her favorites.

Lucas pulled away from the curb. The traffic was light, so getting home shouldn't take long.

"Bella, there is something I need to know before I take you home."

Bella looked out of the window and prepared herself for an inquisition. Surely, there was going to be more questions about why she didn't want to get involved with him. Shit, at that point, Bella didn't even know. Could she simply admit that she was afraid?

"What is that you want to know?"

He graced her with a sexy, lopsided grin and responded with, "Your address."

Bella laughed out loud and rattled off her address. Thankfully, on the way to her house, they enjoyed a light-hearted conversation, which did not include a proposition. Maybe he'd gotten tired of chasing her. Maybe he'd given up. For some reason, Bella was not celebrating the possibility.

After an awkward moment of silence, Lucas pulled over. His eyes were filled with sympathy when he turned to face her.

"What are you doing?" Bella asked him. "What's wrong?"

"I had a talk with Dean," Lucas admitted.

"And?"

"And he told me that he was gay." His tone was low, and his voice was filled with compassion.

Bella couldn't believe Dean's nerve. He'd had no right whatsoever to tell Lucas her business. Bella was sick of him and everyone else telling her what they thought she needed.

Bella threw her head back on the headrest and grunted. The last thing that she needed was pity from Lucas. "Drive the car." Bella's voice had come out hoarser than she'd expected.

CREED 2
by *Phoenix Daniels*

"Bella, listen. I—"

"Lucas, drive the car," Bella gritted.

Bella knew exactly why Dean was constantly interfering in her life. He needed to quell his guilt for leaving her to be with men. He wanted desperately for Bella to find a man...*any* damn man.

Thankfully, Lucas shifted into drive and pulled off. The drive to Bella's house was painfully silent. When Lucas turned on down her block, she was instantly relieved. She didn't want to have a conversation. She didn't feel the need to explain herself.

Lucas parked in the driveway. The burning sensation on the side of her face was an indication that he was looking at her. But Bella ignored his gaze and pretended that undoing her seatbelt was a consuming task.

"Thanks for the ride," Bella muttered.

Bella grabbed her purse from her lap and climbed out of the Land Rover. Without looking back, she hurried up the driveway. She was pulling her keys out of her purse when she heard his car door open and close.

Bella rushed up the steps to her porch. As she fumbled to get the key in the lock, her skin began to tingle, which was always a sign that Lucas was close. Bella unlocked the door, took a deep breath, and turned to face Lucas. She came face to face with his solid chest. He was even closer than she'd thought.

Bella raised her chin to look him in the eye. "Lucas, I don't need you to see me in."

"Do you love him," Lucas asked.

Bella's eyes widened. She definitely wasn't expecting the query. "What?" Bella gasped.

"Are you still in love with Dean?"

Bella tried to step back, but her getaway was obstructed by the door. "Lucas, not that it's any of your business, but no. I've been over Dean for a long time."

"Are you sure?"

"Of course, I'm sure." Bella sneered.

Lucas' eyes narrowed as his gaze roamed Bella's face. He smiled seductively and leaned closer. Bella fought for the strength to resist and turned her head.

"Why do you fight, Bella? I know you want me," Lucas whispered against her neck.

His breath was warm and sweet. It was undeniable, Bella wanted his mouth on her; on all of her. But she didn't trust him. She didn't trust any man. In Bella's experience, they didn't even trust themselves to know who they were or what they wanted. Bella didn't believe that all men questioned their sexuality, but unless they confessed, there would be no way for her to know their truth.

"Bella, I can imagine how—"

"You can't imagine shit!" Bella snapped. "Lucas, you don't even know me. But you think you know how I feel? So, you know how it feels to have *your* husband come home and tell you that he would rather be with a man than you? Do you know what that does to a woman?"

The tears that burned in Bella's eyes made her furious at herself for breaking down in front of Lucas. She swiped at the one that had escaped. "I have made it very clear that I wasn't interested. So, why don't you just leave me alone? Okay, Lucas? Leave me the fuck alone!"

Although her tears had blurred her vision, Bella looked him square in the eye. She was sure that she had finally gotten her point. Lucas narrowed his eyes and grabbed her by the chin. His eyes burned with what looked like rage, and his expression was almost menacing. She'd finally pissed him off?

With his fingers pressing into her skin, he pulled her face closer to his. "You talk too fucking much," he seethed.

CREED 2
by *Phoenix Daniels*

Before Bella knew it or could do anything about it, Lucas slammed his lips against hers. Bella's back hit the door. But she didn't feel pain. She felt overwhelmed. His lips, the way he tasted, his sweet, masculine scent, the way it engulfed her, had rendered Bella immobile.

She gasped. And when her lips parted, Lucas took advantage. He licked the seam of her lips and eased his tongue inside. He teased her tongue with his, and Bella allowed her tongue to reciprocate. She couldn't help the moan that escaped as fire ignited her core.

Lucas released her face and placed his hand behind her head. He was making love to her mouth; making her forget all of her fears. Tearing through her force field was what his passionate kiss was doing to her. Bella snaked her arms around his neck and slid her fingers through his silky hair. The sound of her own moans resonated in her in her head. Bella pushed her throbbing nipples against his hard body, but she simply couldn't get close enough. Lucas palmed her ass and pushed his rock-hard manhood against her softness.

Lucas, lacking any mercy whatsoever, tore his lips from Bella's. "Open the door," he growled.

CREED 2
by *Phoenix Daniels*

Bella reached behind her body and fumbled around until she found the doorknob. When she turned it, the weight of her body caused the door to fling open. She stumbled, but Lucas caught her and lifted her off of her feet. The hem of Bella's dress rose above her thighs when she secured her legs around his waist. Lucas carried her inside and kicked the door closed with his foot. Without the aid of light, he carried her to the middle of the living room floor. He dropped to his knees and gently laid her down on the carpet. The small amount of light coming in through the windows allowed Bella a glimpse into Lucas hungry, emerald eyes. She saw desire. If nothing else, she could tell that it was *her* Lucas desired.

Lucas placed a slow, sensual kiss to her lips. But if Bella thought that he was about to make slow, respectful love to her, she was wrong. Lucas ripped the top of her strapless dress down and sucked her hard, aching nipple into his mouth. Bella gasped loudly, arching her back involuntarily. Her hands flew to the back of Lucas' head. She was pulling him so close that she was surprised that he was able to move. Remarkably, Lucas was able to alternate between both breasts. Bella writhed on the floor as he tormented her nipples. Lucas released a moan from deep down as if Bella's nipples were the sweetest treats that he'd ever tasted. He gripped her breasts, pulling her nipples together and licked from one to the other.

"Mmm, Lucas," Bella purred.

It had been so long since Bella had been with a man. For the longest, she'd avoided sex and relationships. But, at the moment, Bella was unable to let fear or anything else keep her from having Lucas. At the moment, she needed him more than she needed air.

Bella squirmed as he kissed down her body. He glided his tongue down her stomach, and around her navel. Lucas didn't allow her dress to stop his progress. He reached under the hem of her dress and pulled it from under her ass. Lucas tore her panties from between her thighs and tossed them to the side. He eased her thighs apart and kissed his way to her hungry pussy.

Even though Bella was anticipating Lucas' warm, minty mouth on her, she still jerked violently when he closed his lips around her clit. He licked and flicked her swollen bud with an expertise that suggested that he was taking great pride in pleasing Bella.

"Ooooh, yes, Lucas," Bella purred, grinding her pussy against his face. "You're eating my pussy so guuuud."

As if her dirty words were ammunition, Lucas fired at her pussy, lapping, and sucking until Bella could no longer sustain his ravenous blows. Her legs stiffened, her toes curled, and her back arched even more. There was nothing that she could do to stop the bomb of ecstasy from exploding.

"Aghhhhh!" Bella cried, unashamed of the volume of her voice.

Lucas licked her through wave after wave of the orgasm that ripped through her. Bella couldn't remember the last time that she'd had an orgasm that wasn't self-inflicted. Once Lucas was satisfied that he'd consumed every bit of her release, he sat back on his knees and stared down at Bella.

"You're so beautiful, Bella," Lucas whispered on a sigh.

A bead of sweat danced down Bella's forehead. She was panting and on full display in the middle of the floor. Her dress had been reduced to a belt. Bella doubted that the sight before him was all that beautiful, but she didn't care. Bella watched as Lucas unbuttoned his shirt and slipped out of it. Even behind the T-shirt, she could easily see the well-formed muscles of his torso.

Lucas peeled the T-shirt over his head and stood to his feet. He stepped out of his pants and shorts with Bella's full attention. As suspected, Lucas' naked body was a work of art. She followed the deep V until she was admiring the magnitude of his hard, venous dick.

It was beautiful.

Lucas fished a condom from his pocket. He tore it open and tossed the golden wrapper on the floor. Lucas stroked his dick seductively before sliding the condom over it. Bella could hear her own heavy breathing as she squirmed beneath him. It had been so long since she'd been penetrated, and she'd be lying to herself if she said that she wasn't a little nervous about taking in all of his dick.

Lucas dropped to the floor and crawled over Bella's trembling body. She inhaled the virile aroma of Lucas' cologne mix with testosterone. Bella spread her legs and happily invited Lucas inside. He lowered his body to hers, resting on one elbow. With his other hand, Lucas gently swiped a strand of hair from her sweaty forehead. Bella placed her hand on his cheek. She pulled his face to hers and kissed him with a passion that she'd denied herself for so long. Bella licked his tongue and sucked his full bottom lip into her mouth. Out of fear, and maybe a little bit of low self-esteem, she had run from him. So,

CREED 2
by *Phoenix Daniels*

Bella was determined to make him understand just how much she wanted him.

Without breaking their kiss, Lucas pressed his dick against her opening and pushed inside; gifting her with fine steel. Bella inhaled a sharp breath and held it until her body adjusted to the huge invasion.

"Daaaamn, Bella," Lucas rasped against her lips. "Pussy is so tight, baby."

Lucas deepened their kiss, swallowing Bella's moans. He reached down, pulling her knee to his side, and drove into her so deep that Bella accidentally bit his lip. If Lucas was in pain, she couldn't tell. He hadn't missed a single stroke. With every thrust, his already big dick seemed to grow larger. Bella's grinding and grunting and her groaning and moaning intensified as Lucas fucked her into oblivion. Bella clutched the flexing muscles of his back and cried out each time he rocked into her.

"Oh, Go-. Gotdamn, Lucas!" Bella wheezed. "Oh, shit!"

"Aghhh, Bella! I'm making this pussy mine," Lucas declared. "Do you hear me, baby? *Mine!*"

Bella raised her pelvis and did her best to swallow every inch of thick dick that Lucas was offering. Why she had denied herself the unbelievable pleasure for so long, Bella couldn't fathom. Lucas was fucking the shit out of her, and Bella felt the need to return the favor. She pushed at his shoulders and rolled him to his back. Bella climbed on his dick, determined to prove herself worth the wait.

Lucas reached up and grabbed her shoulders. He pulled her body to his until they were sweaty chest to sweaty chest. Bella rolled her hips, shoving herself on his dick as he fucked her from the bottom. Lucas held her head to his shoulders and caressed her back as he slipped in and out her wet throbbing pussy.

Bella savored the sound on his breathy moans and fucked him like he belonged to her. But she wouldn't last. Even on his back, Lucas was mastering her pussy; hitting her G-spot every time he withdrew and rammed back inside of her. Bella raised up slightly and braced her hands on his shoulders. Her entire body was trembling as she bounced up and down on his shaft. Bella pressed her fingers into his muscular flesh. She threw her head back and embraced the orgasm that ripple through her.

"Yes! Yes!" Bella panted. "Aghhh, fuck! I'm cummin'!"

When Bella went limp and fell on Lucas' chest, he gripped her hips and yank her down on his dick. And he kept yanking her until his thrusts frenzied.

"Mmm, baby…sooo good," Lucas groaned. "Your pus-this pussy is milking my fucking cock."

Lucas rammed into her one last time and shouted Bella's name. His body stiffened as he pumped warm semen inside the condom. She could feel his dick throbbing with every ounce released. Their breathing was in sync, and Lucas' pounding heart echoed Bella's.

Lucas wrapped his arms around Bella and kissed the top of her head. Together, they rested on the carpeted floor until they caught their breath.

CREED 2

by *Phoenix Daniels*

CHAPTER SEVENTEEN

TAYLOR

Taylor pulled into her garage and turned the ignition to
kill the engine. She looked back at all the bags in the back seat,
hopeful that she could get them in the house with one trip.
Taylor grabbed her purse from the passenger's seat and climbed
out of her vintage Mustang. She slung her purse strap over her
shoulder, closed the front door, and opened the back door.
Thankfully, Taylor was able to secure all of the bags. Both
hands were full, but at least she wouldn't have to take another
trip. The girls were on their way. And, since she'd had to make
a few runs after their spa day, Taylor was running really late.

She pulled her head out of the back seat and used her hip
to close the door.

"Hello, Taylor," came from a soft, unfamiliar voice from
behind.

Taylor may not have recognized the accented voice, but
she had no doubts about the cold metal pressed to her temple.

"It's nice to finally meet you. Now, sit those bags down
so we can have a nice visit."

CREED 2
by *Phoenix Daniels*

Taylor was plotting a defense strategy. But, her hands were full, her weapon was in her purse, and there was a gun to her head.

"I know what's going on in the head of yours, Taylor. But if you do anything stupid, everyone that walks into this garage will be able to see what's in your head. Now, I need answers that I believe you have. You're coming with me."

It didn't take a genius to figure out that the woman behind her was the same woman who'd abducted Rosemary and viciously murdered Collier and Kara. Taylor was convinced that if she went anywhere with her, she was a dead woman.

"Why don't you ask your questions now? I can answer them. Then, you can be on your way," Taylor proposed.

The woman grabbed a hand full of Taylor's hair and yanked her head back.

"Bitch, you don't set the terms here. *I* do," she hissed. "Put that shit down and let's go."

Overcome by fear, Taylor's hands trembled as she bent to lower the bags to the floor. But, afraid or not, the sight of headlights entering her driveway triggered her fight or flight response. She threw her head back and headbutted her assailant. The woman was shocked for what Taylor was sure would only be seconds. So, Taylor took advantage. She flipped around, grabbed the woman's wrist, and slammed her arm down on her thigh with a force that disarmed her attacker.

Once the woman was disarmed, Taylor threw a punch. But, like lightning, the woman blocked the punch and threw a hard elbow to the side of Taylor's face, knocking Taylor back against her car. She was stunned, but she didn't have time to be dazed. The woman was going for her weapon. Taylor pushed herself off the car and grabbed the woman from behind. She was attempting a chokehold, but the woman caught her arm and performed a wrist lock that brought Taylor to her knees.

'*Goddamn, she's fast!*' is what Taylor was thinking, just before her aggressor lifted her knee, and dropped it down on Taylor's arm. The sound of Taylor's scream didn't drown out the sound of her breaking bone.

Taylor collapsed from the pain. Her face slapped the cold, dirty garage floor. Warm tears spilled from her eyes as she slowly inched toward the woman's discarded gun.

Behind her, the woman laughed diabolically and kicked Taylor's broken arm. Taylor rolled over and grabbed her arm. The pain was debilitating. She'd fought as hard as she could, but it was evident that the woman possessed a skill that Taylor didn't.

The mystery woman kicked the gun away and raised her leg, ready to inflict more pain on Taylor. Scrounging every ounce of strength that she could muster, Taylor prepared to block. Fortunately, for her, she didn't have to. Taylor gasped with relief when a foot connected to the side of the woman's head. When she fell against the wall, Taylor could see that it was Bella who had kicked her.

The woman recovered quickly and threw a punch. But Bella proved to be just as fast. She blocked the punch and delivered an elbow to the woman's face. Bella pulled her gun from her waistband, but it was kicked out of her hand. Both women, clearly trained in martial arts, exchanged lightning-fast blows. Since Bella seemed to be holding her own, Taylor began to look around the floor for the woman's gun. She's found it under her car. Taylor inched closer and stretched her good arm under the car, but she couldn't reach the gun. She rolled over and searched frantically for her purse. There she would find her own weapon. Unfortunately, she didn't see it. What was even more unfortunate, was the roundhouse kick that Bella took to her face that sent her flying. She hit the floor with a loud thud.

And, before she could recover, the woman was standing over her, aiming Bella's own weapon at her. But like a miracle, Victoria swooped in like a savior.

She grabbed the gun from behind and released the magazine, rendering it inoperable. The woman whirled around and swung in Victoria's direction, but Victoria ducked and punched her in the stomach. The woman gasped, clutching her midsection. She was stunned, but she wasn't done. She advanced toward Victoria, and to Taylor's amazement, Victoria smiled as if she was actually enjoying herself. Victoria actually had a weapon on her hip. She could've just shot the bitch. But she was obviously enjoying the hand-to-hand combat. Victoria wanted to break the woman down.

The woman released loud, frustrated grunts as she, unsuccessfully, attempted to deliver strike after strike, and kick after kick. Her every attempt was blocked and returned with a blow from Victoria. For the first time, Taylor sighed with relief. Whereas she was getting her ass beat, and Bella was holding her own, Victoria was beating the shit out of the hit woman. And she was loving every bit of it.

Taylor saw movement from the corner of her eye. She looked over at Bella. She had crawled to her knees and was able to recover her weapon and the discarded magazine. She slammed the clip into the weapon and racked the slide. Bella raised the weapon and waited for the opportunity to shoot the woman without hitting Victoria. Finding an opening wasn't gonna be easy. Victoria was all over her. The skilled hit woman was worn out. Surely, she thought that extracting Taylor would have been easier, but between Bella and Victoria, she'd bitten off more than she could chew.

Victoria leaped from the ground and delivered a brutal sidekick to the woman's throat. When she grabbed her throat and gasped for air, Taylor was sure that Victoria had crushed the woman's windpipe. The woman fell to the ground and struggled to breathe. Since she finally had an opening, Bella raised the weapon toward the killer.

After the ass whipping that Victoria had inflicted, Taylor would have bet anything that the woman was done. But she would have lost that bet. The woman scrambled to her feet and blew past Victoria like the wind. When Victoria took off after her, Bella hurried over to Taylor.

"Tay, are you okay?"

"Ummm…. *Nooo*! That bitch broke my arm!"

CREED 2
by *Phoenix Daniels*

Bella was helping Taylor to her feet when Victoria returned. They both looked up, but Victoria shook her head.

"She got away," Victoria admitted. "That bitch is fast."

"Yeah," Taylor scoffed.

Victoria walked over to Taylor and Bella. She frowned when Taylor winced, clutching her arm.

"What the fuck are y'all into?" Victoria asked, crossing her arms.

Taylor managed a chuckle. A question like that coming from Victoria Storm was hilariously ironic.

CHAPTER EIGHTEEN

BELLA

"What the fuck?!" Lucas exclaimed when he entered the small room in the emergency department.

Since they came together, the triage nurse allowed Taylor and Bella to stay in the same room. Victoria was there too, but she didn't have a single scratch on her. Victoria had mercilessly brutalized a trained assassin. Bella rolled her eyes at the thought. Although she was grateful to be alive, the last thing that she had expected was to have been rescued by Victoria Fucking Storm. What a blow that was. Victoria would surely, never let her forget it.

"Damn," Lucas cursed, hurrying over to Bella.

He gently grabbed Bella's bruised face, lifting it to get a better look. In his eyes, Bella could see the sincerity of his concern.

"Are you okay?"

"Who called you?" Bella asked, turning her head.

"I called him," Victor admitted. "That woman is getting closer and closer to Rosemary. Lucas needs to know what's going on."

CREED 2
by *Phoenix Daniels*

Lucas narrowed his eyes at Bella. "I asked you if you were okay," he stressed in a more serious tone.

"I'm fine," Bella insisted with a huff.

Unable to help herself, she looked over at Taylor. She was sitting in a chair across the room with her arm in a sling, glaring at Bella with a raised eyebrow. Without commenting on Taylor's accusatory expression, Bella lowered her gaze and stared at the floor.

For the first time since he'd entered, Lucas looked over at Taylor. She was far worse off than Bella.

"Oh, my God," Lucas gritted. "Are *you* okay?"

"My arm is broken and my ego is bruised. But, thanks to these two, I'm fine." Taylor chuckled and used her good arm to gesture toward Victoria.

"Lucas, this is my friend, Victoria Storm. Victoria, this is Victor's little brother, Lucas."

"Nothing little about him," Victoria muttered under her breath. She smiled at Lucas and said, "It's nice to meet you, Lucas."

"Likewise. I've met your husband."

Even though there was always a jolt of sexual energy that passed throughout her body when Lucas touched her, Bella managed not to squirm when he placed his hand on her shoulder.

"Great. He'll be tearing through that door—"

With unbelievable timing, Jack pushed through the door just as Victoria predicted. "Victoria?" Jack gasped.

He rushed over to her in a full-out panic and pulled her out of her seat. Jack searched her from head to toe, looking for injuries. Shit, if Jack wanted injuries, he should have been looking at Bella and Taylor.

"Jack, baby, I'm fine," Victoria assured.

He looked her over one more time before pulling her into his arms. Jack kissed her forehead tenderly while caressing the back of her head. The love that he had for her was obvious. He was reacting the same way that Victor had when he first arrived. All of the publicly displayed affection was making Bella feel uncomfortable.

She and Lucas had spent a most incredible night together, but neither of them discussed it afterward. Earth-shattering sex did not equal a relationship. And his being there with her, amongst real couples was awkward.

"We're gonna go," Victoria announced.

Taylor stood and held out her arm for a hug. Victoria walked over and wrapped her arms around Taylor.

As they embraced, Taylor whispered, "Thank you."

"Don't mention it. I'm glad I was there," Victoria responded.

When the women separated, Taylor looked expectedly at Bella.

"Yeah, thanks," Bella muttered.

"You're welcome," Victoria responded dryly, without looking at her.

Jack placed his hand on her back and led her out of the small room. Once the door closed, Taylor looked over at Bella and grinned.

"She saved your ass," Taylor teased.

"And I save yours," Bella shot back.

"Yeah, but you like me," Taylor pointed out through laughter.

Bella rolled her eyes and mumbled, "I did."

Taylor leaned forward, squinting as if she had something on her mind.

"What?" Bella asked, impatiently.

"You and Victoria…"

Bella huffed loudly. "Here we go again," Bella complained.

"Don't you think this beef between the two of you is kinda petty?"

Bella crossed her arms and glared at her friend. "And just what do you know about my beef with Victoria?"

"I know that Donatella is an adult and she can make her own decisions regarding her relationships."

Bella frowned. She was utterly confused. And, by the look on Victor's face, so was he.

"Tay, what the fuck are you talking about?"

Taylor's expression turned to puzzlement. "I thought that you and Victoria fell out because of her breakup with Donatella."

"What?" Bella exclaimed. "Are you serious?"

"Umm, I *was.*"

Bella leaned back in her chair and crossed one leg over the other. "Taylor, I don't sit around worrying myself about who my sister fucks. I could give less than a damn. You're right, Donna is a grown-ass woman. Besides, she wasn't that fuckin' heartbroken by Victoria leaving. She has a tendency to recover remarkably fast."

"Then what is it with you two?" Taylor asked.

Bella stood and turned away from Taylor. She closed her eyes and rested her hands on the wall. "She killed my cousin," Bella whispered.

"What?" Victor gasped.

Bella could hear Taylor's approach. Then she felt her hands on her shoulders. "What did you say?"

"She *killed* my cousin," Bella said through a harsh breath.

"Bella, what are you talking about?"

Bella turned around and looked Taylor in the eye.

"Victoria was kidnapped by some Russians. But that didn't surprise me. Hangin' out with them Sicilians, ain't no telling what kinda shit she's into. But, somehow, my cousin got involved. So, they kidnapped him too."

The look on Taylor's face was that of pure shock. It was the exact same expression that Bella had as she'd watched her cousin's death from the iPad that was mysteriously left on her aunt's front porch.

"Robert, my cousin, was a concierge at the Four Seasons. Apparently, something happened to Natasha. We don't know the whole story, but some kinda way, he was involved.

189

The Russians took him, and some Russian chick forced him to fight to the death, in some makeshift ring. His opponent was Victoria, and she killed him."

"Oh, damn," Taylor whispered.

"Robert's body was found in an abandoned warehouse. And they found the Russian chick's body in an abandoned Family Dollar. She'd been beaten to death. After seeing the video, and watching Victoria fight that assassin, I have no doubt that the dead Russian was Victoria's handiwork.

Taylor frowned. She was confused but sympathetic. "Bella," she started softly. "I'm so sorry about your cousin."

"Thank you," Bella replied timidly.

"But, Bell, as horrible as that is, it seems like Vic was fighting for her life."

"I know, Taylor." Bella sneered. "That don't make me dislike her any less."

Thankfully, sensing that Bella wanted to put an end the discussion, Taylor pulled Bella in for a hug. "I'm so sorry about your cousin, honey," Taylor repeated in a whisper.

Bella gave Taylor a quick pat and nudged her away. She didn't feel quite comfortable showing so much weakness with

Lucas and Victor in the room. Taylor smiled and narrowed her eyes at Bella.

"What?"

"You wanna signed my cast?" Taylor asked with a grin.

"Grow up," Bella muttered, rolling her eyes.

Bella relaxed against the headrest and closed her eyes. When they left the hospital, Lucas had insisted on driving her home. And she was grateful. The soreness had begun to kick in. Bella had been fantasizing about a hot bath since they'd left the hospital. So, when Lucas pulled into the driveway, Bella got a little excited.

Lucas hopped out of the Land Rover and ran around to Bella's side. He opened the door and carefully help her out. Bella wasn't so fragile that she couldn't climb out of the truck on her own, but she didn't feel like a back and forth with Lucas. He'd already proven to be quite stubborn. He clearly wasn't content with taking no for an answer, so Bella kept quiet and allowed him to help.

Lucas held her by the elbow from the driveway to the front door. Bella was laughing inside. The way Lucas was behaving, one would think that she had been blown up in an explosion instead of the good ole fashion beat down that she'd gotten. He was seriously overacting.

Once they were at the door, Lucas held his hand out. Confused by the gesture, Bella looked down at his hand.

"Keys. Give me your keys."

Did Lucas actually think that Bella was too incapacitated to unlock her door? Bella shook her head and handed over her keys. "What about my car?" Bella asked. "It's at Taylor's house."

"I'll get it tomorrow."

Lucas unlocked and opened the front door and ushered Bella inside. Once he closed and locked the door, he grabbed Bella by the shoulders and position her against the wall.

"Stay here. I'm gonna check things out."

"What?" Bella asked with knitted brows.

"Bella, a professional assassin just tried to kill you and your friends. Who's to say that she didn't come back."

"Actually, she went after Taylor, not me," Bella pointed out.

"Yeah, well, now, *you're* on her radar. I'm gonna check the house."

He had a point. Bella nodded her head and allowed him to proceed. Since she was the one with the gun, she would think that he'd allow her to search with him, but Lucas just wasn't the type. She'd been kicking ass and getting her ass kicked for years, but to him, she was just another fragile woman in need of his protection.

If Bella actually thought that the woman was in her house, nothing would've kept her from accompanying Lucas. But there was no doubt in Bella's mind that, after the whipping Victoria had put on her, she needed some recovery time.

"All clear," Lucas confirmed when he re-entered the living room.

Bella pushed off the wall and walked into the kitchen. She grabbed a bottle of white wine from the fridge and two glasses from the cabinet.

"Wine?" she offered.

"Please. Thank you."

Lately, Bella found herself consuming more alcohol than usual. Lucas slipped out of his suit jacket and placed it on the back of the dining room chair. He rolled up his sleeves and leaned over on the island.

"Maybe you should take some time off," Lucas suggested.

Bella poured wine into both glasses and handed one to Lucas. Her aching muscles told her that Lucas was right. "Yeah, I'm gonna take off for a few days."

Lucas made a face that indicated that he was surprised by her compliance. "Really?'

"Yeah. What?"

Lucas shrugged and raised the glass to his sexy lips. As he sipped, Bella replayed memories of the way those lips worshiped her entire body the night before.

"I'm just surprised is all. You seem like one of those people who would go to work with a neck brace on."

Bella laughed. She took a sip from her wine glass and said, "I'm full of surprises, Mr. Creed."

"I see."

Bella raised her glass, emptying the contents. Lucas gave her a strange look when she refilled it. "But I do need to talk to Rosemary tomorrow. How are you two getting along?"

by Phoenix Daniels

Lucas finished his wine and slid his glass to Bella for a refill.

"Rosemary is a pain in the ass," he declared.

Bella laughed and walked over to the fridge. She opened it, praying that there was something inside that didn't need defrosting. She was hungry, but she didn't feel like preparing a gourmet meal.

"Why do you say that?"

"Bella, the woman is bored. My housekeeper and I are her only source of entertainment. When I get home from work, she's right at the door, waiting for me to give her the play by play of my day. And, Alissa, my poor housekeeper can't keep the woman out of her personal life."

"Damn!" Bella chuckled.

"And, to top it off, she's continually badgering me about *you*."

Bella peeped from around the refrigerator door.

"*Me*? What does she want to know about me?"

"Well, not just you," he corrected. "*Us*."

Bella closed the fridge, irritated that she hadn't gone to the grocery store. She returned to the island and grabbed her wine. Hopefully, she could get full from alcohol.

"What about us?" Bella asked.

Lucas smiled and shrugged. "I've known Rosemary for a long time. Before Taylor came along, she was the sister that we'd never had. For a long time, she's been on me to settle down."

Bella smiled. She didn't know Rosemary at all, but judging by the way Victor and Lucas talked about her, she wasn't a bad person. She did have an air of privilege and entitlement. But she *was* privileged. So, was her attitude really her fault? What Bella did know was that the woman's presence was creating a problem for her friend.

"Lucas, what does that have to do with me?"

"Well, Belladonna, Rosemary believes that you and I are meant to be," Lucas reported with a grin.

"Is that so? And she believes this *because?*"

"Girl, a blind mute can sense how I feel about you."

Bella chuckled. "That is so politically incorrect," Bella admonished.

Lucas smiled and lifted the glass to his lips. "Well, it's a good thing I'm not the politician in the family."

Bella laughed. And, even though she was tempted, she avoided asking him how he felt about her. As a matter of fact,

CREED 2
by *Phoenix Daniels*

she'd made it point not to discuss the night that they'd shared. After their mind-blowing sexual encounter, she'd fallen asleep on the living room floor. But, the next morning, she woke up in her bed, with Lucas doing the most incredible things to her with his very talented mouth. After another round, Bella made them a breakfast that consisted of toast and coffee. Bella kept the conversation casual until it was time for her to go to work. They hadn't spoken since until Lucas showed up at the hospital.

Lucas placed his glass on the countertop and stood straight.

"Bella?" he called, hesitantly. His tone was concerning.

"What's up?"

"Can I have your phone number?"

Bella was surprised by his request. The man had licked every part of her body and he didn't even have her phone number. Their shit was ass-backward, Bella mused.

"Sure." Bella chuckled.

"Good. You can have mine too," Lucas responded with a boyish grin.

"Okay."

Lucas walked around the island and pulled Bella close to him. Bella looked up into his sparkling green eyes and rested her hands on his well-developed biceps. Lucas leaned down and pressed his soft lips to hers. He gave her a quick, gentle kiss that made Bella melt against him. He pulled back and looked her in the eye.

"I'm glad you're okay," he whispered.

"Me too."

When Lucas stepped back, Bella felt an instant loss. She was suddenly cold.

"Finish your wine. I'm gonna run you a bath. Then, I'm going to bathe you. Then, I'm going to put you to bed. And then…" he said, giving her another soft peck.

Bella's core tingled and her nipples tightened. She was filled with erotic anticipation.

"And then?" she asked.

"I'm going to massage and kiss every part of your body."

Lucas' voice was deep and sensual. Bella would be lying if she said she wasn't excited about the idea of Lucas taking care of her.

BLACK WIDOW

Sloane stepped out of the shower and limped over to the small sink. She wiped the steam from the mirror and winced at the sight of her battered face. She had greatly underestimated the governor's girlfriend. She was a fighter. Even though Taylor Montgomery was no match for Sloane, she was able to catch her off guard and disarm her. The detective, on the other hand, was a skilled fighter. Putting her down took a bit more work.

However, Sloan definitely wasn't expecting Taylor's friend to step in and completely overpower her. Sloane had put down men twice her size. But Taylor's friend was so much more than an expert. She fought with a skill set and the passion of a woman possessed. Sloane was nowhere near a match for the woman. Her overconfidence had gotten her ass beaten and her shoulder dislocated. Sloane was able to snap it back into place, but she was going to need weeks of recovery.

She wrapped the cheap scratchy towel around her aching body and left the bathroom. She flopped down on the hard mattress and looked around the cheap motel room. She was disgusted by the place, but she couldn't risk being captured on camera in the expensive hotels that she preferred.

CREED 2
by *Phoenix Daniels*

Sloane needed to regroup and she needed to produce results. The client was getting impatient, and her reputation was on the line. She didn't know why Rosemary Creed needed to die, and she didn't care. Sloane never asked why a target was a target. The reasons were irrelevant to her. But getting the job done was taking more effort than Sloane had expected. After the ass whipping that she'd received, she realized that trying to find and kill Rosemary Creed might just be the death of her.

CHAPTER NINETEEN

VICTOR

"It's time, Governor," Renee Griffin, Victor's press secretary announced.

"Ugh!" Victor grunted.

Renee smiled and shoved the list of talking points in his hand. "You'll do fine," she assured. "You always do. You're handsome, and the people love you. Hell, half the time, they don't even listen to what you're saying. Folks just like looking at you."

"Bullshit," Victor scoffed.

"I gotta go out there and sugar coat the fact that the moron before me butchered the fucking budget so bad that I have to support a ridiculous tax and claim that it's for their own good. These people can see right through this shit. Listen here, lady. I pay you to bullshit them, not me."

Renee laughed and patted Victor on the shoulder. "Come on. We got this," she said over her shoulder as she walked into the press room.

Renee walked up to the podium. After a few words at the microphone, she announced to the press that Victor would be taking their questions. Victor checked his tie and walked over the podium. Renee smiled and took position behind him. After a quick greeting, Victor allowed the first question.

"Governor Creed, how do you justify the Sweetened Beverage Tax? Government officials claim that a penny per ounce is supposed to dissuade consumers from purchasing sweetened beverages, but all it seems to be doing is sending shoppers to bordering states."

As suspected, even with all the other shit going on in the world, the first question was about the beverage tax. It's a damn shame that the county board of directors couldn't come up with a better solution. In his opinion, if they trimmed a little fat and were less frivolous with spending, they would have the money for vital county services. In a perfect world, their question would've been directed at Tara Periwinkle, the county board president.

"It's simple, Jerry," Victor told the reporter. "Pop is bad. The county is broke. It's an inherited problem. So, I have to allow the county to sort it out. The truth is, this tax will generate at least 200 million dollars a year that will go toward keeping vital public services from shutting down."

"So, will cutbacks on government spending!" one reporter shouted.

The reporter was right. The budget had been blown to bits by excessive spending and bad management. Now, the taxpayers were expected to clean up the mess. Victor didn't back the tax, but the outcome didn't match his opinion. But he was no fool. Victor would bet his business that the tax was going to be repealed. For the county board president to try to convince the people that the tax was to prevent diabetes and childhood obesity, and not simply to generate revenue, showed a complete lack of insight to her constituents' intelligence. Victor didn't want to touch the subject at all.

"Agreed. Government spending should be audited. But auditing takes too long. We're dangerously running the risk of having to close down our public health facilities."

Victor brought his hands together and steepled his index fingers. As instructed by Renee, he leaned over on the podium. She had told him that the gesture went over well with constituents. This simple gesture was meant to make him seem more engaging.

CREED 2
by *Phoenix Daniels*

"Governor Creed, how do you respond to the Commander in Chief blaming both sides for the unrest in Charlottesville?"

Victor's brows knitted. He stood straight, contemplating his response. He knew that Renee wanted him to steer clear and disassociate himself from the stupid shit that the president often said. But Victor being Victor decided to engage.

"I believe our Commander in Chief should stifle his remarks and stop making all Republicans look ridiculous."

Victor looked back at Renee. A rumble of laughter from the crowd didn't stop her from giving him the eye. Victor shrugged and turned back to his audience.

"And let me say this: Over the last several years, the black community has been pushing back against the racism that has been a pustule on this country since its beginning, while white people pat us on the back for how progressive we are and how far we've come. However, since the 1960's, black people have been saying that we still have a long way to go. There is still work to be done, and we're not doing it.

Black people are rightfully tired of that work being left undone. And they will not let us ignore it anymore. And do you know what? Our collective response as white Americans has been a blatant example of precisely what the black community is protesting.

We tell the black community that they need to be peaceful and undisruptive if they want to be heard. Never mind that Martin Luther King's marches blocked traffic or that social change in this country has almost never happened without public demonstrations that got big enough and loud enough so as not to be ignored. When people of color protest, we call it a riot and bring in riot gear. Peaceful protesters at Standing Rock were met with violence by with police in military gear. Neo-Nazis in Charlottesville, Virginia were merely supervised by police in standard uniforms. And, when one the neo-Nazis killed a counter-protester, people ironically said that they shouldn't have disrupted the demonstration."

Victor paused to take a breath.

"Bear with me. I'm in speech delivering mode." Victor chuckled, reaching for the glass of water that was placed aside for him.

He took a sip and held up one finger to ensure that the crowd remained quiet. He replaced the glass on the table beside the podium before he continued.

CREED 2
by *Phoenix Daniels*

"But it is Black Lives Matter that is 'too violent' and 'too disruptive' and therefore, they don't have a message worth hearing. When they can behave themselves, we'll hear them out. The message has been undeniable: If people of color, particularly, *black people* want to be heard, first they should be quiet.

When members of the black community kneel during the national anthem, we scream over the disrespect toward the flag. The black community can protest, we say, but they need to find another way to do it. We don't like this way.

People, you're not supposed to like it. It's supposed to make you uncomfortable and draw your attention. That's what protesting is. And guess what? It's working. It has people all over America, even the world, talking. Now, it's up to *us* to listen, understand, and fix it.

Instead, we are, as always, debating the means of protesting rather than the purpose. We call it unpatriotic even though protesting injustice is about as patriotic as you can get. We say that quietly kneeling is a slap in the face to veterans who fought for our freedom, conveniently ignoring the fact that our freedom includes the freedom to kneel.

CREED 2
by Phoenix Daniels

We are collectively more upset about disrespecting our flag than we are about people being treated as second-class citizens and shamefully, often being killed. We're willing to hear them out and fix the problem, we say, but only when the black people find a better means of telling us about the problem that we already know about.

At the end of the day, when the concern over respect for a flag is greater than our concern for people's lives or when it's even an issue when people are saying, 'stop killing us', we're shining an ugly light on ourselves. Instead of standing with people who feel so disenfranchised by their own country that they can't stand for the flag, we demand respect from a group of people who've been stomped on for generations before we'll consider not stomping on them anymore.

I say this to my fellow Americans, if you're angry about people kneeling during the National Anthem, maybe it's time to stop and think about how marginalized and angry they have to be to refuse to stand. Think about the pride you have in your country, and then be ashamed of how that country treats some of its own people. We *are* that problem. And it's time for us to do something about it instead of policing the tone of the people who are suffering."

CREED 2
by *Phoenix Daniels*

Victor, not expecting to the room to erupt with applause, sighed and took a step back from the podium. Renee stepped up a whispered in his ear.

"You love to make me earn this money, don't you?"

Victor turned to her with a smirk. "That's why you get paid the big bucks," he teased.

"Great speech, Governor, but your white brethren are gonna be gunning for you."

"Fuck 'em," Victor muttered.

Victor and Renee's conversation ended when the room when eerily silent. The sound of phones ringing and buzzing reverberated throughout the press room. That kind of buzz meant a breaking story.

"Go, now, Governor," Renee urged.

If it was breaking news and they both knew that any statements made or answers to questions would be unprepared and straight off the cuff.

Victor turned and hurried out of the press room. But not before he heard a reporter shouting at his back.

"Governor Creed, did you know that your wife was alive?"

CREED 2
by *Phoenix Daniels*

Stunned by the question, Victor stumbled, thankfully, out of view of the cameras. He was rushed into a small office by Gregor. Renee was on his heels. In the past, she had never been anything but composed. But, as she stared at the breaking story on her iPad, her demeanor bordered around panicky.

"Governor, please tell me that you are just as shocked as I am. Tell me that you didn't know anything about this," she demanded.

Victor couldn't lie. "I knew she was alive," he admitted.

"What the fuck?!" Renee exclaimed.

Victor was taken aback. He'd never heard his press secretary use profanity. She was the epitome of calm rationality.

"What the fuck am I doing here? Why wouldn't you tell *me*? This is some bullshit, Victor!"

Yep, that calm rationality shit just went out the window.

Victor knew that Renee was fuming because it was the first time that she'd addressed him so informally. She tossed the iPad on a table and pulled out her phone. She dialed hysterically and pressed the phone to her ear. "Cameron, my office now!" she shouted into her phone.

Cameron was Renee's assistant. She ended the call and stuffed her phone in her briefcase. She turned to Victor and sat down in a chair at the table. Renee inhaled a deep breath and then exhaled it. After gathering her composure, she grabbed the iPad and handed it to Victor.

Victor looked at the picture and gasped. "What the fuck is…what the fuck is she doing?"

"She's shopping at Tiffany's," Renee scoffed.

"I don't…I gotta make a call."

"First, I need you to tell me *everything*," Renee requested calmly.

*****

Gregor and his team ushered Victor through the sea of reporters from the Thompson Center to the dark SUV. They were hammering him with questions about Rosemary so much so as to suggest he'd forced her to fake her death so that he could gain a sympathy vote in the election.

Once he was safely tucked inside the vehicle, Victor pulled his phone out of his pocket. He needed to warn Taylor about the fallout. Renee climbed in next to him and Gregor hopped in the passenger's seat.

"Take me to Lucas' place!" Victor barked at the driver.

"No." Gregor intervened. "I'm sorry, Governor. Your wife just put a huge target on her back. We won't be taking you there."

Victor ran his fingers through his already mussed hair and leaned back in his seat. He was worn and not in the mood to fight with his head of security.

"Can we summon them?" Victor asked in compromise.

"Yes, sir, we can work that out," Gregor conceded.

"Great," Victor muttered.

Victor hit the number two, speed dialing Kena. When she answered, he could tell by her tone that she'd seen the news

"Kenyatta, I need you to call Lucas, my other brothers, and Detective Devereaux right now. Tell them to meet me at the penthouse."

"Yes, sir."

"Oh, and Kenyatta?'

"Yes?"

"You tell Lucas that if he has to drag Rosemary by her hair, I want her in my apartment ASAP."

"Will do, Governor," she softly replied. "Umm, do you need me there?"

"Yes."

"Are you okay?" The sound of real concern was bleeding from her voice.

"Yeah, I will be. Go on. Get it done. I'll see you in a few."

"Yes, Governor."

CHAPTER TWENTY

BELLA

Bella poked her head into the autopsy room, which was NiYah's domain.

"You rang?"

NiYah looked up with a smile despite the fact that she was holding a human brain.

"Yeah, come on in."

Bella frowned. I don't want to. I hate it in here. It smells like old death and emptiness.

"Old death and emptiness?" Bella chuckled. "Da fuck does emptiness smell like?"

"It has a smell," Bella quipped.

"I got work to do here."

Bella was used to dead bodies. But, watching NiYah carve them open, she could do without.

NiYah placed the brain on a scale and returned to the body that she was working on. She was face deep in guts. Without looking up, she said, "I have something for you."

CREED 2
by *Phoenix Daniels*

Bella took one last breath of unscented air and walked into the autopsy room. She stood over the open cadaver, one of her female victims.

"Can't you just call me?" Bella complained.

"Oh, my God, Bella. You see dead bodies all the time."

"Yeah, but not their spleens!" Bella exclaimed. "What do you have for me?"

NiYah looked up at Bella and rolled her eyes. She covered the decedent with a sheet and pulled off her gloves.

"Well, for starters, that barcode was linked to a human trafficking ring from a few years back. It was run by some Russians." NiYah washed her hands and walked over to a work table.

"How do you know this?" Bella asked.

"There were several women found in a van a few years ago. They were all logged with the same type of barcode. These women were mostly Eastern European."

"Logged by whom?"

NiYah flipped through a couple of pages in the file. "It says here, Officer Natasha Walker and Officer Steven Shaw."

CREED 2
by Phoenix Daniels

It had all come together for Bella. Natasha, Victoria, Robert, and her three dead girls were connected to the same criminal enterprise. Shamefully, Bella had avoided launching a real investigation into Robert's death. She knew that her cousin was into some shady things. And, for the sake of her aunt, Bella didn't want to drag Robert's skeletons out of the closet. Truthfully, it was just easier to blame Victoria and her associations.

"There's more," NiYah added, interrupting Bella's thoughts.

"Okay?"

"Well, that beauty over there," NiYah said, pointing to the dead girl. "She fought back. We pulled DNA from her fingernails and teeth."

Bella instantly became excited. "Did you—"

"Send it to the lab? I did," NiYah interrupted with a wide smile. "I rushed it. *And* I got a hit!"

Bella felt like dancing. She would have hugged NiYah if she wasn't covered in dead juice.

"NiYah, NiYah, NiYah, you are the shit!" Bella squealed.

"I tried to tell ya," NiYah joshed. She pulled a file from a cabinet and handed it to Bella.

"Happy hunting, Detective."

If Bella could prove that the three dead girls were somehow linked to Rosemary, she could close both cases. The DNA profile couldn't have come at a better time.

*****

The uniformed officer walked over to Bella's desk. He was stuffing his handcuffs back in the case on his duty belt.

"All good?" Bella asked.

"Yeah. He's in interview 3."

"Thanks, Todd," Bella said with a smile.

She was outright giddy. She'd promised Lucas that she would take a few days off, but Bella hadn't expected NiYah to hand her suspect. She couldn't resist going in. She stood, grabbed a file folder and her notepad, and happily made her way to the interview room.

Bella opened the door and stepped inside. She smiled and placed the file and the notepad on the table that separated her from her suspect. He was handcuffed through a metal loop

216

in the table. His irritation was evident as he shifted in the hard metal chair.

"Michael Anderson, I'm Detective Devereaux.

"Maybe *you* can give me some answers. Why the hell am I here?"

Bella was happy to explain. She took a seat across from him, opened the file, and showed him photos of the three dead girls. The look on his face told Bella that he had a fairly good idea as to why he was there.

"I will tell you this, Mr. Anderson: You have the right to remain silent. Anything you say can *and* will be held against you in a court of law. You have the right to an attorney. If you cannot afford an attorney, one will be provided for you. Mr. Anderson, do you understand your rights? And with these rights in mind, I'd like you to realize exactly how fucked you are."

CREED 2
by Phoenix Daniels

CHAPTER TWENTY-ONE

BELLA

Bella sat patiently in the chamber of The Honorable Judge Jessica Franklin. She was waiting for the judge to finish reading the warrants that she'd prepared. She was going over them with a fine-tooth comb. After all, it wasn't every day that a warrant request to arrest a senior United States senator as well as warrant requests to search his home and office were placed on her desk. But Bella had crossed all T's and dotted all I's. Michael Anderson, Henry Craven's security chief, had sung like a canary when Bella revealed that it was his DNA on the dead girl. His loyalty to the senator clearly hadn't overshadowed his basic need for self-preservation.

While she waited, Bella turned to the judge's television. Victor was giving a news conference.

"May I turn that up a bit, Judge."

The judged looked up at Bella and then over to the TV.

"Oh, sure. I've been waiting for this press conference."

She grabbed the remote from her desk and turned up the volume. She was about to return her attention to the warrants until Victor made an unflattering comment about the president. He went on to address the protests during the national anthem.

Victor's eloquent condemnation of those offended by the players' peaceful protest made Bella proud to know him. It was about time more white people stood up against the injustices inflicted on black people and other people of color. Bella looked over at the judge. And Bella had suspected that as a black woman, she agreed.

"Oooh, that *man*," The judge crooned, closing her eyes. "Mm… mm…mmm."

Bella laughed at the judge's lascivious behavior.

Judge Franklin opened her eyes and giggled. "Girl, I wish I could summon that Caucasian to my chambers, so I can have my way with him. That Taylor Montgomery is one lucky sistah."

 Bella didn't comment, she was too busy staring at a picture of Rosemary Creed shopping on Michigan Avenue.

What the fuck?!

When Judge Franklin reached for the pen on her desk, Bella was elated. But she needed to call Taylor. No one told her that they were gonna reveal the fact that Rosemary was alive.

CREED 2
by *Phoenix Daniels*

The judge signed the warrants. She stood and handed them to Bella. "Go get that son of a bitch, Detective," she hissed.

*****

Bella threw the driver's door open and hopped out of her car with enthusiasm. She couldn't wait to put handcuffs on the crooked senator.

Sergeant Carver climbed out of his unmarked vehicle and walked over to Bella. "You ready for this?"

"Real ready," Bella quipped.

The tactical team that was lent to them by the watch commander began to pull up. Once they were out of their cars, Bella pulled them in for a huddle. They were divided into three teams: the entry team, security, and the search team. Two uniformed officers were to post up out front. Bella was going in with the entry team. She wanted to see the look on the senator's face when he realized that life as he knew it was over.

One of the larger tactical officers went to his car and pulled out a battering ram and a Chicago bar out of the truck. They didn't have a no-knock warrant, but they wanted to have tools on the ready in case the senator refused to open the door.

CREED 2
by *Phoenix Daniels*

Just as they approached the property, three additional cars pulled up. Bella's lieutenant, her commander, and the superintendent climbed out of each. Bella turned to her sergeant with narrowed eyes and pursed lips.

"What? I had to tell my supervisor. I guess he told his," the sergeant defended with a shrug.

Bella turned back to the house, ignoring the presence of the bosses. Since they hardly ever participated in the execution of a warrant, Bella was sure that they were only there, hoping for a photo op.

The entry team hurried up the long driveway. Bella followed close behind. Once they were near the massive double doors, the team fell to the side. Bella walked up and knocked hard on the door.

Less than a minute later, a small African American woman opened the door. "May I help you?"

"We're here for Senator Craven," Bella announced as she walked past the woman.

"The senator is in the shower!" the woman shouted. "What is this all about?"

One of the entry team members grabbed the woman by the arm and pulled her aside.

CREED 2
by *Phoenix Daniels*

"Who else is in the house?" he asked her.

She stumbled as he dragged her into another room. Bella walked across the foyer.

"Search everything!" she yelled over her shoulder.

Bella found a staircase and climbed them to the top. Just as she turned down the hall, the senator burst through one of the doors wearing only a robe.

"What the hell is going out here?" he bellowed.

"Senator Craven, you're under arrest for pandering, human trafficking, and conspiracy to commit murder."

The senator turned as white as a sheet. There was no disguising the fear in his eyes. He knew that his time had come. "What?" the senator gasped, stumbling against the wall. "What are you talking about?"

"Michael Anderson, Senator."

"What about Michael? He's part of my security!" barked the senator.

"He gave you up," Bella revealed with a satisfied grin.

At the sound of that, Senator Craven clutched his heart and dropped to his knees. Bella pulled out her cuffs. She walked over and stepped behind him, pulling his arms behind his body.

Bella read him his Miranda rights as she secured the cuffs around his wrists.

The feel of the cold metal must have snapped the senator out of his state of shock. "What are you doing? I am a United States senator! You can't do this to me!"

Bella pulled the senator to his feet and dragged him down the hall. Once they were downstairs, she handed him off to one of the security officers. The officer placed the senator on the sofa with his housekeeper and his weeping wife. Bella was curious to know if the senator's wife knew the sadistic shit that her husband was involved in. She would be sure to question the woman later.

Bella joined the others. They searched the senator's large house from top to bottom. Three hours later, they were placing evidence in plastic, department-issued bags. Bella had found more than she'd ever expected. Apparently, the senator was quite paranoid and he certainly didn't trust his co-conspirators. He recorded all of their conversations. There must have been more than a hundred audio recordings and some video. It was definitely going to take a while to sift through all of it.

Bella went to take one of the evidence bags to the car, but when she walked past the room where the senator had been placed, he wasn't there. Bella walked into the room. His wife had buried herself in the corner of the sofa, and the housekeeper was sitting next to her with folded arms and pursed lips.

"When can I go?" she asked, impatiently. "I don't live here."

Ignoring the woman, Bella turned to one of the officers. "Where is the senator?" she asked.

"The new guy took him to the bathroom."

Bella walked out of the room and down the hall. When she reached the bathroom door, it was open and empty. Bella sat the bag on the floor and jogged up the stairs. An officer that she didn't recognize was standing in the hall. She figured that he must have been the "new guy."

"Where is the senator?"

"He's getting dressed."

Bella looked over at the closed bedroom door and prayed that the idiot hadn't left him alone.

"Who's in there with him?"

The officer gave Bella a puzzled look. "Nobody. He's getting dress."

He actually said it with a "duh" connotation.

"You stupid motherfuckah!" Bella barked.

She ran over to the door and tried the knob. It was locked. In a panic, Bella kicked the door until it flew open. She entered the room in just enough time to see the senator eat a bullet.

"Goddamn it!" Bella screamed.

CHAPTER TWENTY-TWO

TAYLOR

Victor hurried Taylor through the swarm of reporters that had been camped out at her house since Rosemary revealed that she was alive. He ushered her into the back seat of the SUV and climbed in after her. Earlier, he'd called and told her to pack a bag because they were going to be staying in the penthouse indefinitely. Taylor was already packed. After seeing the news, she was expecting the call. She instantly went from being immensely proud of her man to shocked and horrified by the sight of Rosemary coming out of Tiffany's.

"Governor, your wife, and brother are waiting for you at your apartment," Gregor informed.

Hearing him refer to Rosemary as Victor's *wife* was like taking a bullet.

"Thank you, Gregor. Has anyone been able to reach the detective?"

"No, sir."

Victor turned to Taylor. "Have you talked to Bella?"

"No. I tried calling her, but her phone went straight to voicemail."

226

CREED 2
by *Phoenix Daniels*

Victor ran his fingers through his thick hair and blew out a frustrated breath. Taylor used her index finger to turn Victor's face toward hers. Once they were eye to eye, Taylor smiled. "Hello," she said with a raised brow.

Victor closed his eyes and sighed. "Aw, baby, I'm so sorry," he whispered. "Hi. How was your day?"

"It was cool. I went to see my parents. When my dad saw my cast, he was ready to kill somebody." Taylor chuckled.

"Yeah, I know how he feels," Victor muttered.

He draped his arm over Taylor's shoulder and pulled her into the nook. Taylor inhaled the familiar scent of the man she loved.

"I love you," he whispered.

"I know you do, babe."

Taylor relaxed against Victor until they arrived at Storm Tower. They waited behind the shielding of the tinted windows until Gregor and his team secured the area. Once they were escorted out, Gregor and his team shielded them from reporters. He ushered them inside the building and tucked them into the elevator. They were ascending to the penthouse when Victor turned to Taylor with a concerned look in his eyes.

"What?" Taylor asked.

CREED 2
by *Phoenix Daniels*

"I think we should stay at the mansion for a while."

Taylor didn't mind spending weekends in the governor's mansion, but she didn't want to live there. It was so big and very far from everyone and everything that was important to Taylor. From the moment Victor found out that she'd been attacked, she knew that he was going to suggest that they retreat to Springfield.

"Baby, let's deal with one thing at a time," Taylor said as the elevator doors opened

Victor gave her a look that said that he knew that she was avoiding the subject. Taylor grinned and exited the elevator. Victor opened the door, and as soon as they stepped inside, they were practically bum-rushed by Rosemary.

"Victor, hear me out," she started.

Taylor looked past Rosemary to Lucas' angry face. He took a sip from the glass he was holding and shot fiery darts at the back of Rosemary's head.

"What the fuck were you thinking, Rosemary?" Victor admonished.

"Look at Taylor!" Rosemary shrieked. "I can't keep putting the people that surround me in danger. Taylor and her friends could've have been killed, Victor!" Rosemary shook her head emphatically. "I'm sorry, but I just can't live with that."

"So, you threw yourself out there as bait?" Taylor asked.

"Yes. I won't have another person's death on my conscience, especially not the people that I love."

Taylor cleared her throat.

"I don't believe that Lucas was even on this woman's radar, and Victor has more security than the royal family. I know you're not throwing yourself out there because *I* got hurt."

"But I am, Taylor." Rosemary sighed. "I know that you don't know me very well, but I love Victor so very much, and he loves you. Like, he's *in love* with you. He deserves that. And I'll have nothing to do with taking that away from him."

Admittedly, Taylor was touched. Victor had told her that they were never in love, but to hear her say it was sort of solidifying. "You shouldn't have put yourself in danger. My friends and I can take care of ourselves."

"You shouldn't have to," Rosemary argued

The room went silent when a man from Victor's security staff entered the apartment with Taylor's bags.

"I'll take the bags," Victor said. "You can leave them there. Thank you."

What's done is done, Taylor thought. There wasn't a thing that Victor, Lucas, or anyone else could do about the situation that they were in. The cat was definitely out of the bag.

"I called my dad," Rosemary announced. "I explained everything. When he gets his security team in place, he'll be coming to get me."

"So, you'll risk your *father's* safety," Lucas muttered.

"I tried to refuse, but he insisted."

Victor and Lucas shared worried looks.

"Well, I'm gonna go take my bags to the bedroom."

"No, babe, I got the bags," Victor said, hurrying over to Taylor.

"Nope. I got 'em. Y'all handle things here." Taylor grabbed her bag from the floor, tossed the strap over her good arm, and dragged roll-aboard across the beautiful marble floor. But, before she could make it to the hall, the front door opened, and Gregor walked in.

"Governor, Detective Devereaux is here to see you."

Taylor sat the bag down and left the roll-aboard. She walked over to the door, anxious to see Bella. She'd been calling her all day. Bella walked into the penthouse with a smile on her face.

"We've been calling you all day," Victor snapped, wiping the smile right off Bella's face.

Bella crossed her arms and shifted her weight to one leg. "Governor, I'm not your woman. You need to watch your tone with me."

Taylor recoiled as if Bella had just slapped her. "But *I* am. So, you watch your tone when you talk to him," Taylor retorted.

Bella's eyes grew wide. She looked at Taylor as if she'd lost her mind.

"*He* started it!" Bella shrieked.

"*He* is my fiancé, and *he* is also the governor of Illinois. Show some respect, friend."

Bella blew out a harsh breath and uncrossed her arms. "I had good news. I don't even know if I wanna tell your asses now," Bella mumbled with a roll of her eyes.

"Victor," Lucas called out in a stern voice.

Victor turned to Lucas with a questioning glare. Lucas stood to his full height, folded his arms, and nodded toward Bella. Victor turned to Bella.

"My apologies, Detective."

"Thank you. I'm sorry for being so snappy."

After Bella accepted his apology and apologized, she went on to them all about her day with the senator.

If the senator was dead, Rosemary was no longer in danger, and they could all breathe a sigh of relief. On the other hand, there could have been more people involved. Not to mention the infamous black widow. What if her ego was bruised by the good ole fashion beat down Victoria had served her? She could come back just for the hell of it.

"Okay, since Rosemary's dad is in the process of hiring more security, why don't we just keep her close for now?" Taylor proposed.

"You mean, I can stay here with you guys?"

"Uh, no," Taylor, scoffed. "Victoria said that if need be, you can stay in one of the apartments here. Since you're still married to Victor, he can assign you a security detail." Taylor turned to Victor with a smirk and added, "*Legally*."

Everyone in that room knew that Taylor often times had an unofficial security detail. And, now that she'd been attacked, that detail would more than likely be permanent.

CREED 2
by *Phoenix Daniels*

"Oh, and you should stay with Lucas," Taylor suggested with a sly grin.

Bella ignored Taylor and turned to Victor. "Governor Creed, do you mind if I pour myself a drink?"

"Come on in the rec room. I'll have Vera fix us all some drinks. We need to celebrate your brilliant detective work."

BELLA

Victor and Lucas were having a conversation at the bar while Bella sat on the sofa with Rosemary and Taylor. Vera, the housekeeper, walked in with an ice bucket containing a bottle of champagne. She placed it on the bar in front of Victor.

"You know he's crazy about you?" Rosemary whispered.

Bella assumed that the question was rhetorical, so she didn't answer. She was too busy watching Vera flirt shamelessly with Lucas. Bella had never seen anyone take so long to open a bottle of champagne. Thankfully, Lucas' behavior was nothing more than polite. Unfortunately, his indifference only served as fuel for the woman's advances. She started to find reasons to touch his arm, place her hand on his back, or place her hand over his. Lucas finally figured out the woman's play and retreated to the other end of the bar. When it looked like Vera was trying to inch her way closer to him, Bella hopped up from the sofa, walked over to Vera, and grabbed the bottle of champagne.

"Don't get fucked up," Bella warned the flirtatious domestic.

CREED 2
by *Phoenix Daniels*

Bella popped the cork, poured champagne into a glass, and handed it to Lucas. She poured her own glass, narrowed her eyes at the housekeeper, and walked back over to the sofa. She left the woman with a terrified look on her face.

"That'll be all, Vera. Thank you," Taylor told the housekeeper.

"Yes, ma'am," she replied before scurrying out of the recreation room.

Bella looked up and Lucas. He was donning the silliest grin. Surely, his head was swollen from watching Bella mark her territory. Or he could have very well been thinking, *'How the hell did she go from I don't want you, Lucas, to I'll beat a bitch's ass?'*

Bella rolled her eyes at Lucas and looked over at Taylor. "You need to get rid of that trick," Bella warned. "She's gonna be walking around naked in front of your man soon."

"I concur," Rosemary mumbled. "She won't let *me* stay, but she'd allow that tart in her house?"

Taylor rolled her eyes and got up to pour her own champagne. But, when she looked back, Bella could see that she and Rosemary had put something on her mind. It was almost a guarantee that Miss Vera was as good as gone.

CHAPTER TWENTY-THREE

BELLA

Bella was on her belly, stretched across Lucas' enormous bed, listening to yet another set of audio tapes. Over the last few weeks, Bella had learned that Senator Craven had been an intricate part in the human trafficking racket for years. He'd made millions exploiting women and even children. She'd also proved that the senator was in fact involved with the organization that'd had a hand in the kidnapping of Natasha, Victoria, and Robert. Henry Craven's death was not the close of Bella's case.

Over the last three weeks, Bella had made thirteen arrests based on evidence from the senator's house. And there were more to be made. Bella wasn't nearly done. She was going to identify every voice on those tapes.

The voices on the tape turned into *blah, blah, blah* when Lucas walked out of the master bathroom with a towel wrapped around his waist. The combination of his gorgeous face and chiseled body was distracting, to say the least. His dark hair was wet and slicked back from his handsome face. And his striking green eyes were gleaming with desire. Bella had been staying at

CREED 2
by *Phoenix Daniels*

Lucas' place for the last three weeks, and she was still in awe every time he got naked.

Lucas strolled over to the bed and stood in front of Bella. She was up close and personal with the large bulge beneath the towel. She inhaled the exotic mixture of soap and raw masculinity. Lucas kneeled until they were face to face. He smiled and pecked her lips before pulling the headphones from her ears.

"Hey," he said in a sexy baritone whisper that meant the promise of pleasure.

"Hey," Bella replied with a smile. "How was your shower?"

"Hot," he said in another sensual whisper.

Bella was tingling with anticipation. She rose up on all fours and pulled the towel from Lucas' body. Bella suddenly had a carnal desire to be the source of his pleasure.

CREED 2
by Phoenix Daniels

LUCAS

Bella tossed Lucas' towel to the floor and climbed off of the bed. The lustful look in her dark eyes was hypnotizing.

"Come with me," she urged in deep, sensual tone.

She grabbed his hand and led him away from the bed. Lucas didn't know where she was taking him and he didn't care as long as she provided relief for his painfully swollen cock. As she led him across the bedroom, Lucas admired the sway of her hips. She was wearing only a T-shirt and panties. Her perfectly round ass was peeping from under the hem of the T-shirt. Lucas was imaging her on all fours, her sweet pussy swallowing his cock.

Bella led him to the other side of the room and position him so that he was facing the armoire. Lucas was puzzled, but he kept quiet. He'd let her have her way as long as her way ended in eruption for them both.

"Put your hands up there."

As instructed, Lucas placed his hands on the top of the armoire. Bella stepped back and slowly peeled the T-shirt over her head. When her gorgeous tits bounced from under the T-shirt, Lucas wrapped his arm around her waist and pulled her to him. Bella's pert nipples, surrounded by large, dark areolas, were a temptation. Lucas longed to put his mouth on her. But Bella gave him the stiff arm and a stern look.

"I said, put your hands there," she admonished with a sinful grin.

However, impatient, Lucas returned his hands to the top of the armoire. Bella smiled and dipped under his arm so that she was standing in front of him. She freed her silky, black hair from the high bun, enabling it to cascade down her bare shoulders. As he looked down at her, Lucas concluded that Bella was the most beautiful woman that he'd ever seen. She wrapped her arms around his neck and stood on her toes. Lucas kept his eyes on her plump, sexy lips until they joined with his. A sigh escaped from the simple connection.

Bella's kiss was sweet and sensual, sending erotic currents straight to his cock. Had she not instructed him to keep his hands on the armoire, he would've squeezed the shaft to relieve some of the ache of his need. When his angry cock began to throb, Lucas groaned against Bella's lips.

"Bella," he grumbled.

She lowered herself to her shorter height and looked up at him. She was torturing him, and the smirk she was wearing told him that she knew it. What she didn't know was that Lucas was about to turn her around and fuck her against the cabinet. But, just as he'd resigned to do so, Bella wrapped her small fingers around his cock. Lucas gasped from the sensation of her touch. Their eyes locked and maintained contact as Bella slowly lowered to her knees. Without looking away, she wrapped her sweet, wet lips around his eagerly, pulsating dick. When Bella sucked the swollen head into her hot mouth, Lucas' knees weakened. To stay on his feet, he braced himself against the armoire. He was staring down at her. And she was staring up at him with a hunger in her eyes that made Lucas want to feed her.

Bella tightened her soft fingers around his shaft and began to stroke. She folded her lips, tightly around his cock and used her mouth to shadow the movement of her hand. Bella was slurping, sucking, and stroking Lucas into hysteria. She was mastering his cock. As his dick throbbed in her mouth, Lucas knew that he wasn't going last much longer.

"Aghh, fuck! Bella!" Lucas roared.

Unable to help himself, he ripped his hand from the armoire and gripped the back of Bella's head. As he fucked her face, his full, heavy balls tightened. Lucas' knees locked, his legs stiffened, and his cock was nearing an eruption.

CREED 2
by *Phoenix Daniels*

Heavy breathing and feral growls echoed throughout his bedroom. Lucas slammed his fist on the top of the armoire and whimpered like a wounded animal as his cock pumped hot cum into Bella's mouth. His entire body jerked violently with every ounce of semen that pulsed from his dick. His breathing hitched each time he heard Bella swallow. Out of breath, Lucas collapsed against the armoire, resting his head on his arms.

"Bella," he croaked, out of breath. "Oh, Bella..." Lucas worked on controlling his breathing and regaining the strength in his legs. "Oh, fuck," he panted, pushing himself of off the armoire. Lucas reached down and pulled Bella to her feet. He wrapped his arm around her waist and pressed his forehead to hers. "Baby, you are... Oh, baby."

Lucas gave up on speaking and held her against him until he was sure that he could walk. Savoring the feeling of Bella in his arms, Lucas was in no hurry, because he had every intention of honoring her tight pussy all night.

CHAPTER TWENTY-FOUR

BELLA

Bella was applying her lipstick in the mirror of Lucas' gigantic bathroom. He walked up behind her and smacked her on the ass, causing her to jump and smear lipstick on the side of her face. Bella frowned at Lucas in the mirror. He laughed and handed her a tissue. As Bella wiped her face, Lucas pulled the headphones from her ears.

"You're becoming obsessed," he warned.

"Yeah, you're probably right," Bella admitted. "But there is so much going on with this case."

"Bella, sweetheart, that case was closed when the senator died. You've created a dozen more cases for yourself."

"Lucas, I'm telling you they're all related."

Lucas wrapped his arms around her waist and pulled her back to his chest.

"Maybe they are. But, right now, we're gonna be late for dinner."

Bella rolled her eyes. She would've preferred to stay in and watch TV or better yet, continue listening to the senator's tapes. But she and Lucas were taking Rosemary home to her dad, and she had insisted that they stay to have dinner with her and her father.

Lucas kissed the side of Bella's face and smiled in the mirror. "I have an idea," he mumbled against her face.

Bella covered his hands with hers and melted against his chest. "I'm listening."

"Well, since you're off the next couple of days, I was thinking that after dinner we could drive straight to my family's lake house in Benton Harbor, Michigan. It's quiet, secluded, and less than two hours away. We could get a *whole* lot of quality time in."

The look in his eyes told Bella exactly what Lucas meant by *quality time*. Bella turned around in his arms, snaked her arms around his neck, and kissed him on the chin. "Okay. Let's do it."

Lucas' brows furrowed. He seemed surprised that Bella had agreed so quickly. Hell, Bella was surprised that she'd agreed so fast.

"Really?"

"Really," Bella affirmed.

Lucas' smile prompted Bella's. For some reason, she loved being the source of his happiness. For the last few weeks, he'd definitely been the source of hers.

Bella stood on her toes and gave him a quick peck. "Now, move. You done fucked up my makeup."

She gave him a gentle shove and turned back to the mirror. She grabbed the lipstick, and just as she was about to reapply it, Lucas slapped her ass again.

Bella whipped around. "Lucas!"

She was ready to attack, but Lucas had already fled from the bathroom in a fit of laughter.

✱✱✱✱✱

"So, sweetheart, how does it feel to be home?"

"It feels amazing. I have missed you so much, Daddy."

Phillip Bloomberg smiled at Rosemary and covered her hand with his. They were seated at the dining room table waiting on one of his many young housekeepers to serve dinner. The wealthy lobbyist seemed to have surrounded himself with young, beautiful women. Bella looked around, amazed by Phillip's Barrington home. It was massive, especially for a man who lived alone. Rosemary had told her that her mother had died during childbirth and her father had chosen to never remarry. So, she wondered why a person would need so much space.

Bella took a sip of the nastiest wine she'd ever tasted. She would bet her paycheck that the bottle was worth more than her paycheck. She looked over at Lucas. He was rich, so maybe it was a rich people's thing. The frown on his face caused Bella to chuckle. Apparently, money couldn't buy taste.

"Lucas, I'd like to thank you for keeping my little girl safe."

Lucas placed his wine glass on the table and nodded. "Rosemary is family," he told Phillip. "We take care of family."

"Yes," Phillip agreed.

He went on to talk about his own family. He mentioned how his beloved wife had died giving birth to Rosemary. If Bella wasn't mistaken, she could sense a hint of resentment in the older gentleman's tone. But she was no psychiatrist, so she kept her observations to herself. She did, however, take notice of how familiar Phillip seemed.

Bella sat quietly, battling with her memory as Phillip's housekeepers finally served dinner. She was staring, and she knew it. But Bella couldn't help herself.

CREED 2
by *Phoenix Daniels*

"Is everything alright, Detective?" Phillip asked, obviously noticing that Bella was staring.

Bella blinked out of her haze and cleared her throat. "I-I'm sorry, Mr. Bloomberg. You just seem so familiar to me," Bella admitted.

Phillip smiled and sipped more of the nasty-ass wine. "That's because we've met before," Phillip revealed.

Bella was confused. She and the stupid rich didn't hang in the same circles. Well, other than Victor and Lucas. But, then again, there was Jack and Victoria. Because of Taylor, they seemed to bump into each other often.

"Yes," Phillip continued. "We met at Victor and Taylor's pre-engagement party."

Bella smiled. It had come back to her. They were introduced at Taylor's private engagement party; the one that she and Victor had held at Taylor's house.

"That's right," Bella reminisced. "I remember now."

A young pretty server placed a salad made with arugula and a bowl of lobster bisque in front of her. Bella picked up her soup spoon and stirred the soup. It didn't have much substance, just tomato sauce, and corn. But it smelled really good. Bella tasted the soup and decided that she would stick to the salad.

CREED 2
by *Phoenix Daniels*

Over the next thirty minutes, Bella endured a mediocre meal. She couldn't help but wonder if the bland meal was the result of Phillip being Caucasian or rich. Again, she looked over at Lucas for a reference. He was both rich and Caucasian. And, again, the frown on his face made her chuckle.

Lucas leaned over to Bella and whispered in her ear. "We'll get tacos on the way home."

Bella nodded and raised the napkin to her lips. She needed something to hide her laughter. She looked over at Rosemary. The woman had been living in Louisiana for years. Surely, she wasn't content with tasteless food. Sure enough, Rosemary hadn't touched the food on her plate.

Phillip tossed his napkin over his plate and leaned back like a man who had just enjoyed a hearty meal. "Let's have a drink in the parlor, shall we?" Phillip grunted.

Bella was starving. She wanted to get out of the pretentious mansion so that she could get something decent to eat. Hopefully, Popeye's was still open.

"Thank you, sir, but we wouldn't dream of keeping you any longer. We're gonna be going. Thank you for dinner," Bella said, graciously.

"Nonsense," Phillip argued. "Come with me." He stood and walked toward the arched doorway that led to the parlor. "Right this way," he instructed.

Lucas stood and straightened his tie. He held his hand out for Bella. She reluctantly put her hand in his and stood from her seat. She looked up at Lucas, pleading with her eyes for him to rescue her from the evening.

Seemingly, reading her mind, Lucas looked over at Phillip Bloomberg. "Phillip, Bella and I are gonna call it a night. It's been an eventful couple of weeks, and we have a weekend planned."

Phillip seemed as if he wanted to convince them otherwise, but Rosemary mercifully intervened. She hurried around the table to Bella's side. She grabbed Bella by the hand and rubbed her forearm.

"Daddy, the lovebirds have a getaway planned. We mustn't stand in their way. We'll dine again together soon."

Phillip wasn't moved. His demeanor was strange. Bella couldn't pinpoint why, but he seemed to be stalling. All of a sudden, the hairs on the back her neck stood straight up. It was like a Spidey sense had been activated. Something wasn't quite right. For some reason, Bella sensed danger. And, then, it came to her. Bella knew exactly why Phillip seemed so familiar to her. And it wasn't from Taylor's pre-engagement party.

It was from the tapes!

CHAPTER TWENTY-FIVE

BELLA

Rosemary's father was on the tapes that Bella had confiscated from Senator Henry Craven's house.

Phillip Bloomberg, the wealthy lobbyist, was one of the voices on many of the tapes. So, it was more than reasonable to believe that he had something to do with hiring a professional to kill his own daughter.

Bella pulled her hand from Lucas'. As discrete as she could, she slipped her hand into her purse. Her plan was to grab her gun and get her, Lucas, and Rosemary out of the house as fast as she could. Bella had no idea what kind of muscle Phillip had in the massive house.

"The gangs all here," a feminine voice taunted from behind.

Bella whipped around and nearly stumbled at the sight of the woman from the restaurant and Taylor's garage.

Lucas had only seen the woman briefly. But since she and Rosemary had had physical encounters, they gasped at the same time. Bella could only imagine how confused Lucas must have been, but she couldn't take the time to fill him in on what was happening. She kept her eyes trained on the threat in front of her.

Bella was able to get a good grip on her weapon. She didn't pull it out of her purse because she didn't want to set the violent woman off. She planned to wait for an opening and take her best shot. Unfortunately, her target was already pointing a weapon in their direction.

Bella knew that the woman had no problem taking them all out, so she needed to stall.

"So, it was *you*," Bella directed at Phillip. "You commissioned the death of your own daughter."

Phillip narrowed his eyes and crossed his chubby arms across his chest. "She means nothing to me!" Phillip spat, heartlessly.

"*Daddy?*" Rosemary gasped, painfully.

"Shut up!" he seethed. "I won't lose another thing over you!"

Tears filled Rosemary's sad blue eyes. She was completely taken off guard by her father's hateful declaration. Learning that the monster that she'd been running from was her own father had to be devastating.

"No, Daddy, please don't tell me you—"

"Didn't he say shut up?" The woman interrupted. "You are a pathetic, naïve little brat! This is the real world, princess. Your *daddy* could care less whether you live or die. He's a *monster*. Did you know that? Your daddy sells children. He makes his money off the backs of the weak. Did you know that?"

The woman shook her head and frowned as if she was repulsed by the idea.

"I didn't know that either. You see, I *am* a hit woman, and I *do* kill people for a living, but I have *never* asked why a person needed to be hit. I carry out jobs with no questions asked. But, after running across Taylor Montgomery and her cop friends, I did a little research. For years, your father here has enslaved young and even *underage* girls *and* boys. He sells them for profit. Just look around this house. Every last one of his servants is a victim of human trafficking."

Bella kept her mouth shut during the killer's rant and eased her gun from her purse. She stepped in front of Lucas. But Lucas placed his palm to her side and forced her behind him. Gun or no gun, Lucas planned to keep Bella out of the line of fire.

"Daddy, no," Rosemary whimpered.

Phillip gave the murderous woman a stern look. He didn't seem pleased by her description of him. "Kill her!" he ordered.

CREED 2
by *Phoenix Daniels*

Bella froze when the woman fired her weapon. She fired a round but not into Rosemary. She shot *Phillip*. She put a bullet right in his head. The shocked look remained on his face as he fell. His dead body made a loud thud when it crashed on the hardwood floor. Rosemary screamed.

Bella was shocked as well. The woman turned her gun to Rosemary and said, "Sadly, I have known many like your father. They don't deserve to breathe. Unfortunately for you, I have never missed a target, and I won't start today. I'm sorry, but you gotta die too."

Rosemary was crying hysterically, staring at her father, but she didn't say a word. She simply dropped her head as if she had resigned to her fate. She seemed content and ready to die, but the killer diverted the direction of her weapon from Rosemary to Bella and Lucas.

"No witnesses," the killer declared.

Bella dropped her purse to the floor and pointed her gun at the hit woman. Her intention was to end her. But, surprisingly, Rosemary leaped in front of her and Lucas just as the woman pulled the trigger. Her leap into the line of fire shielded Bella from the bullet that was meant for her. The look of sadness and betrayal on Rosemary's face would probably haunt Bella forever.

CREED 2
by *Phoenix Daniels*

"Oh, fuck!" Lucas gasped.

He caught Rosemary before she could hit the floor. He held her close to his chest and lowered her gently to the floor. Bella aimed her weapon and fired at the assassin. Blood spurted from the killer's chest, but she wasn't down.

Unfortunately, Bella was. When she fired, so did the woman. Bella had been hit in the chest. Her breath hitched, her heart raced as her body went limp. The pain was indescribable. It was like fire. Bella had no control over her limbs. Even though her life didn't flash before her eyes, she had a feeling that her life was over. She'd wanted so much more for her future, but the life she lived was the one she'd chosen. Bella thought of her family. She thought of her friends. But the idea of what her life could have been with Lucas was saddening.

At the sight of Bella's wounded body, Lucas gasped and tossed Rosemary aside. He caught Bella in his arms and grabbed her weapon with his free hand. But the assassin wasn't done. She fired at Lucas hitting him in the shoulder. But Lucas was strong and determined. With the speed of lightning, he pointed the .45 at the female assassin and shot her right between her eyes.

For a second, Bella took solace in the fact that the killer was down, but she was having trouble focusing. She couldn't command her body to do anything. She couldn't move her limps. Her breathing was labored, and she was weakening by the second. And it was cold...so cold that her body trembled involuntarily.

Lucas crawled over her and promised that she would be okay. But Bella knew that wasn't true. She suddenly thought of her twin. Could Donatella feel her pain? Could she sense that Bella was dying? Lucas pressed his palm against her wound. He was pretending to be calm, but Bella could tell that he was panicking.

"You're okay," he assured with a whisper.

The way he looked, like a lost little boy, made Bella want to make everything okay for him. She clutched the hand that he had on her chest and did her best to smile.

"I know, baby. T-thank...thank you. I-I...I'm okay," she promised.

Lucas pulled his phone out of his pocket. As he called for help, Bella closed her eyes. She was so tired. She could fight no more.

CHAPTER TWENTY-SIX

BELLA

The sound of something scraping against the floor caused Bella to stir. Her eyelids fluttered in a struggle to open.

"Welcome back, sleeping beauty," a familiar voice whispered in the darkness.

Bella's eyes flew open. Without moving her body, her eyes roamed the room.

I'm alive! Thank God!

Bella looked around and realized that she was in a hospital. She said a silent prayer to thank God before focusing on her unexpected visitor.

"Victoria Price," Bella mumbled in a weary and hoarse tone. She wasn't too weak to fuck with Victoria.

"*Storm*," Victoria corrected.

"Whatever. What are you doing here? Where are the people that I actually care about?"

"Now, is that any way to talk to the woman who saved your ass?" Victoria asked, smiling down at Bella.

"Ha," Bella scoffed. "Where were you when this hot lead went through my chest?"

256

"I can't be everywhere now, can I?"

Not in the mood to entertain the witty tete-a-tete with Victoria, Bella closed her eyes and whispered, "Lucas."

Regrettably, it was clear that Rosemary was dead. But, before she lost consciousness, Lucas was very much alive. Bella needed to see for herself that he was okay.

"Your boyfriend is in surgery. He should have had surgery yesterday when you were brought in, but he refused to go under until he knew that you were going to be okay. He'll be fine. Your family and very large extended family is in the waiting room. The doctor said they could visit when you woke up."

"Then, how the hell did you get in here?"

"I'm rich and over-privileged." Victoria chuckled.

"It must be nice to have snagged a rich man." Bella snickered.

"Yes. Yes, it is. Is it nice for you too, Bella? Because the last time I checked, Lucas Creed was the Stanford-educated, genius, millionaire CEO of Brothers' Creed Incorporated."

Bella chuckled and regretted it immediately. She cringed from the sharp pain in her chest. "What do you want, Victoria?" Bella grunted.

CREED 2
by *Phoenix Daniels*

Victoria leaned over Bella's bed. Her expression turned serious. "We need to talk."

The change in Victoria's demeanor caused Bella to worry. She was attempted to sit up when Victoria placed a firm, but gentle, hand on her shoulder. Having no other choice, Bella calmed and relaxed against the pillow.

"What is it, Victoria?" she asked in a frightful whisper.

"Taylor reached out to me."

"And?"

Victoria's eyes were filled with sadness. Bella clutched to bedrail with anxious anticipation.

"Robert," Victoria said softly.

Bella breathed a sigh of relief. She was afraid that Victoria was about to deliver devastating news. Since she hadn't, Bella closed her eyes. She was unwilling to grapple with Victoria about the death of her cousin. "Not now, Victoria."

"Bella, I need you to know that I didn't want to fight your cousin. They had my family and they were using them to make me fight. I had no choice," Victoria explained.

Bella opened her eyes and looked up at Victoria. She could see the emotional distress that Victoria was battling as tears streamed down her face. It was obvious that she had been severely scarred.

"Vic—"

"Wait, Bella. I-I am so sorry," Victoria apologized, sobbing. "I *had* to fight for my own survival, my family, and my unborn—"

Victoria's head fell. She cried openly, clinging to the bed sheet as if she were holding on for dear life. Even though Bella had seen the video, she'd never allowed herself to imagine what the ordeal must have been like for Victoria. But, once she did, her own tears threatened to fall. She placed her hand over Victoria's and pried it from the bed sheet. Bella held her hand and whispered, "I know."

Victoria sat in the chair that she had dragged over to the bed. She rested her head on the bedrail and attempted to compose herself. Bella allowed her to grieve in silence. She held her hand, hoping to bring her some sort of comfort.

After a minute or two, Victoria wiped the tears from her cheek and looked at Bella. "I need to thank you," Victoria told her.

Bella swiped at her own tears and frowned.

"*Thank me?*" Bella was confused. "For what?"

"All along, I knew the Russians couldn't run an operation like that in the U.S. without help from someone within the U.S., but I was never able to find the connection. What happened to me and Robert was a devastating taste of hell. *Everyone* needed to be held accountable." Victoria paused and blew out a cleansing breath. She squeezed Bella's hand and looked her in the eye. With noticeable sincerity, she said, "Thank you for being a good detective."

Grateful for the compliment, Bella smiled up at Victoria. She accepted her apology for killing her cousin as if Victoria had been given a choice in the matter. "Vic, you've been through hell and back. We're good."

Victoria raised a brow at Bella. "Shi-id! I ain't ever been shot, bitch," she snorted. "How are you feeling?"

Bella rolled her eyes and snatched her hand away from Victoria. "I feel like I've been shot, stupid."

Victoria stood and dragged the chair into a corner. Branding a mischievous grin, she turned back to Bella. "By the way, your sister is here," Victoria informed with a raised eyebrow. "She's looking *real* good."

CREED 2
by *Phoenix Daniels*

"Look, bitch, you done fucked my sister and killed my cousin. How 'bout you just stay away from my family so that I don't have to fuck you up?"

Victoria laughed and held her hands up in surrender. "Fair enough," she acquiesced.

"Good. Now, get out and send somebody in here that I like."

Victoria walked over to the door and opened it. "Your wish is my command," she said before she slipped out of Bella's room.

Bella was feeling groggy, no doubt from painkillers. She was having trouble keeping her eyes open. So, she gave in to her body's demands and allowed her eyes to close. Bella figured that if she took a short nap, she would have more strength and energy when Lucas came out of surgery. She wanted to be there for him when he woke up.

Bella slept until a light, glowing through her closed lids, disturbed her rest. Her eyes fluttered open. So much for a quick nap.

"Hey, Belly."

Bella blinked up at her twin sister. She was almost unrecognizable. They were as different as night and day.

CREED 2
by *Phoenix Daniels*

Whereas Bella wore her hair long and straight in a more traditional native style, Donna was rocking a short, edgy pixie cut. Donatella had at least seven tattoos, and Bella had none. If they didn't share the same face, one wouldn't dream that they were twin sisters.

"Hey, Telly," Bella rasped. Bella cleared her throat. She winced, not expecting the action to be so painful. "I wanted to get a little nap so I can be up when Lucas gets out of surgery."

Donatella frowned and tilted her head. She was looking at Bella like she'd lost her mind, and Bella wanted to know why.

"What? Why are you lookin' at me like that?"

"A little nap? Girl, Lucas got out of surgery *last night*. He's been parked over there ever since."

Donatella pointed across the room. Bella turned her head and slowly shifted her body so she could see the other side of the room. The sight of Lucas asleep in a hospital bed with an IV taped to his wrist made her heart skip a beat.

"How long have I been out?" Bella asked.

"Um...for at least twelve hours."

Bella was amazed. It truly felt as if she'd just closed her eyes. "How is he?"

by *Phoenix Daniels*

"High," Donatella mused. "Every now and then, he'll jerk awake and hurt himself and then call out your name. With wild-eyed craziness, he looks around the room. And, when he looks at you and realizes you're okay, he goes back to sleep."

Bella smiled. His big body was barely fitting into the small hospital bed.

"In about five minutes, he gonna jump up and look for you. It's so cute." Donatella sighed.

Bella returned to her comfortable position and looked up at her sister. Since Donatella worked undercover, she hadn't spent much time with her in the past months.

"How are you, Telly? I've missed you."

Donatella leaned over and rested on the bedrail. She used her thumb to swipe a renegade strand of hair from Bella's forehead. She smiled down at her twin. "I've missed you too. All you had to do was call me. You didn't have to get shot in order to see me."

"Well, now, I know," Bella scoffed.

Donatella looked toward the door and then back to Bella. She smiled with wide eyes. "Bitch, the governor is out there!" Donatella giddied.

CREED 2
by *Phoenix Daniels*

Because she had a feeling that it would hurt, Bella suppressed a chuckle. She had spent so much time around the governor as of late until she'd become accustomed to his presence.

"He is Tay's fiancé," Bella pointed out.

"Girl, and his fine-ass *brothers*… I want one," Donatella declared breathlessly.

Bella shook her head at her sister's brashness. "Umm…don't you have a man?"

"Bitch, fuck him!" Donna blurted out. "Jack Motherfuckin' Storm is out there too!"

A laugh escaped before Bella could stop it. Her sister's presence was so comforting that even the pain in her chest was tolerable. Donatella was on a roll. She closed her eyes and raised her hand to the sky, no doubt about to continue to express her approval of the alpha-male testosterone floating around the waiting area.

"Not only that, Belly. Victoria was looking—"

Thankfully, Donatella's declaration was interrupted when the hospital door opened. Lincoln, the younger Creed brother, stuck his head in the door.

"Is he up?" he whispered.

"Yes!" Donatella lied.

Bella cut her eyes at her deceitful, desperate little sister. "No, he's not, Lincoln. But you can come in."

Lincoln entered the room and held the door until it closed so as not to make much noise. With his eyes never leaving Donna, he walked over to Bella's bed. He leaned over and kissed her forehead. Since she'd only come in contact with Lucas' brother a few times, she was surprised by the display of affection. He looked down at her with his brother's green eyes and smiled.

"How are you feeling, Detective?"

"I'll live," Bella grumbled.

"I'm glad. My brother made quite a scene until he was sure that you were going to be okay."

Bella smiled because she wasn't surprised. Besides, the fact that his bed was next to hers gave her a feeling of peace. "I don't doubt it," Bella scoffed.

"Well, Bella, you look great. I hope you're feeling up to visitors because I gotta warn you. My parents and the rest of my brothers are outside getting ready to invade your space."

"You tell them that Bella needs her rest," Lucas rasped to Bella's surprise.

CREED 2
by *Phoenix Daniels*

All heads turned in his direction. He was sitting up in bed with his arm in a sling. His dark hair was falling wildly around his face, and he had a five o'clock shadow that made him look dangerously alluring. His hospital gown had fallen off of one shoulder, exposing his strong bicep. Bella was sure that no one else in the room was affected by Lucas the same way because the sight of him made her heart skip a beat.

"Lucas," Bella said breathlessly.

Lucas lifted the sheet and climbed out of bed. He looked well for a man who had recently come out of surgery. With a sexy grin, he walked over to Bella. He placed his warm hand on her cheek. Relishing in the pleasure of his touch, Bella closed her eyes and rested her face on his hand.

"How's my girl?" he whispered.

"Alive and happy to see you."

Bella opened her eyes and reached for Lucas' face. She looked into his stunning green eyes and surmised that she had to have been completely nuts to push such a beautiful man away. Fear had ruled her. And it was that fear that would've caused her to miss out on someone so wonderful.

"Kiss me," she demanded softly.

CREED 2
by *Phoenix Daniels*

Without hesitation, Lucas leaned over and placed his lips on hers. Bella moaned from the pleasure of his tender kiss.

"Awwwwe, y'all so cute," Donatella crooned.

Sadly, the sound of the hospital door opening prompted Lucas to sever their connection.

"Well, I see somebody's feeling better."

Bella looked over to find Lucas' mom standing in the doorway.

"I'm fine, Mom," Lincoln joked.

"Shut up, boy! I'm talking to your brother."

Lucas stood upright as him mom crossed the room. But, to Bella's surprise, she bypassed Lucas and headed straight for Bella.

"I'm so glad you're okay," she said softly. She smiled and cupped Bella's face in her hands.

Bella covered her soft hands with her own. "Thank you, Mrs. Creed."

Tabitha Creed had beautiful skin, a beautiful smile, and eyes the color of the Caribbean Sea. She narrowed those pretty eyes as if she were in deep contemplation. "You are gonna give me some beautiful grandbabies someday," she queried.

"Mom!" Lucas barked. "Are you trying to make her get up and run out of here?"

Bella laughed, clutching her sore chest immediately afterward. "Mrs.—"

"It's *Tabitha*, dear."

"Tabitha, Lucas and I just started seeing each other, so can we hold off on the babies for now?"

Tabitha smiled down at Bella and gently rubbed the top of her head. "For now," she whispered with a mischievous glint in her eye.

"You're up!" a voice yelled from the doorway.

Bella froze at the sound of her mother's voice. She looked at Lucas and hoped that he didn't see the panic in her eyes. Bella was definitely not looking forward to her parents meeting Lucas or his family. In both of their communities, Native American and African American, the "white man" was the oppressor.

Tabitha graciously stepped aside as Bill and Winona Devereaux made a beeline to Bella's bedside. Her mom looked down at her with a troubled expression.

"Baby, how are you?"

Bella tried to reassure her mother with a smile. "I'm good, Mama."

Winona kissed Bella's forehead. "Are you sure?" she asked in a whisper.

"I promise. I'm fine."

Winona looked from Bella to Donna and shook her head in disgust. Her expression turned quickly from worry to agitation. "Between you two and that damn police department, I'm just a nervous breakdown waiting to happen," she fussed.

"Why are you lookin' at me? I didn't get shot," Donatella squealed. "I'm the *good* twin."

Bella, her mom, *and* her dad glared at Donatella with disbelief.

"What? I am!" she exclaimed.

Bella chuckled and rolled her eyes at her lying sister. Since her mom was already irritated, Bella decided to rip off the proverbial bandage and introduce Lucas to her parents. Lucas eased around his mom when Bella held her hand out for him.

"Mamma and Daddy, this is Lucas Creed. And this is his mom, Dr. Tabitha Creed, and his brother, Lincoln."

Lucas smiled and extended his good arm to Bill. Bella held her breath and prayed silently that her dad would accept his hand. Bella sighed with relief when her dad smiled and grasped Lucas' hand.

"Daddy, Lucas is Bella's boyfriend," Donatella added.

Bella cut her eyes at her shit-starting twin sister. If she were healthy, she'd be tempted to smack the silly grin off of her face.

"It's nice to meet you, young man," Bill greeted enthusiastically.

"It's my pleasure, sir."

"Bill. Call me Bill," her dad insisted.

Lucas nodded his compliance and turned to Bella's mom. "Mrs. Devereaux, it's so nice to meet you."

Bella's eyes grew wide when her mom rushed up to Lucas and grasped his good shoulder. She smiled up at him, and Bella instantly felt sorry for him. She could tell that he had no idea how to respond.

"You and my Bella could make *beautiful* babies," her mom predicted.

Bella's mouth flew open. She was absolutely mortified. Lucas squinted and graced her mother with his adorably sexy, lopsided grin.

"You really think so?" he asked her.

"Lucas!" Bella scolded.

CREED 2
by *Phoenix Daniels*

"What?" he argued with a shrug. "My mom said the same thing. They both can't be wrong,"

"Excuse me, everyone," Bella's dad asserted, drawing everyone's attention to him. With a true fan's excitement, he smiled wide and pointed to the hallway. "The governor is out there!" he announced, enthused. "And a senator too!"

Bella laughed with everyone else at her dad's fanatic enthusiasm. For some reason, it hurt a little less than it did before. "Daddy, the governor and the senator are out there because *he* is in here," Bella explained, gesturing toward Lucas.

Winona shook her head at her husband's silly behavior and walked over to Tabitha. Maybe since they shared the same motherly concern and relief that their children were alive and well, the women greeted with a hug.

"So, this is where you moved the party," Victor said from the doorway.

He held the door open so that Taylor and his father, Victor Senior, could enter. No more than thirty seconds later, Lucas' other brothers, Alexander and Jaysen, walked in. The small hospital room was bursting at the seams with family. And just when she thought that no one else could fit in the room, Dean

271

rushed in. He hurried over to Bella, clutched her face in his hands, and kissed her forehead.

"Whoa! Back up, big guy. That's my brother's lady," Lincoln warned, grabbing Dean's arm.

Dean stiffened and looked down at Lincoln's hand on his arm and then right into Lincoln's eyes. The look in Dean's eyes was nothing short of menacing. And, If Bella wasn't sure, she would swear that Dean growled.

"Dean..." Bella whispered sternly.

She was maybe the only one in the tiny room that had seen Dean lose control. Gay or not, he was very protective...very alpha.

"Hold on," Lucas intervened, grabbing Lincoln's arm. He pulled his brother back and walked over to Dean. "Stop kissing my woman," Lucas scolded.

Dean turned to Lucas with narrowed eyes. "*Your woman?*"

"My woman," Lucas verified, confidently.

Dean may not have noticed, but Bella sensed that the Creed brothers were super alert and ready to pounce. Dean was big and he was strong, but so were the Creeds—all of them. Bella attempted to sit up. She was worried for her ex-husband and friend.

Dean looked at Bella for verification. "You his woman?" he asked.

The entire room went silent, waiting for Bella to respond. "I...we...well...we're...yes. Yes, I am."

Dean's expression turned soft. Bella could see the approval in his eyes as he smiled. "That's *wonderful*, Bells," he said with a sincere expression. He grabbed her hand and squeezed gently. He looked back at Lucas. "No kissing your woman," he promised.

Lucas laughed and patted Dean on the back. "Good shit," he responded with a smirk. "Come here. Let me introduce you to my family."

Bella relaxed as she watched how everyone in the room was interacting. Introducing Lucas and his family to her family had turned out much better than Bella had expected.

CREED 2
by *Phoenix Daniels*

CHAPTER TWENTY-SEVEN

BELLA

SIX MONTHS LATER…

"Detective, your two-block perimeter has been set. Headquarters has a command center set up just outside of that perimeter. All teams are in place and ready to go. They'll hit when you make the call. 10-4?"

Bella brought her radio to her mouth and pressed the call button. "10-4, squad. Is ICE, EMS, Fire, and Social Services in place?"

"10-4. All agencies are on scene."

"Thanks, squad."

Bella stuffed the radio into her back pocket and walked over to her car. She reached in and grabbed her ringing phone from inside the vehicle. She smiled when she realized it was Lucas calling. She swiped the screen and held the phone to her ear.

"Hey, babe. What's up?"

"I just wanted to remind you to be careful and to tell you how proud I am."

CREED 2
by *Phoenix Daniels*

Lucas' voice warmed her all over. Bella turned around and leaned against her car. "Awe, shit! You proud of me, bae?" Bella beamed.

"Of course, Belladonna. You're making the world a better place."

Bella squinted at the dark SUV that pulled across the street. She pushed off of her car when the occupants stepped out of the vehicle.

"Thanks, honey. But I gotta go."

"Okay. Be careful."

"I will."

"I love you, Bella."

Bella ran her fingers through her hair and exhaled. She loved when Lucas told her that he loved her because she knew that he meant it.

"I love you," she whispered.

She disconnected the call and stuffed her phone in her bra. Bella crossed the street and walked over to the SUV. She smiled as she approached Victoria and her cousin, Natasha.

"Hey, y'all. Glad you could make it."

"Hey, Bella. Thanks for the invite."

"You deserve to be here. Both of you do."

CREED 2
by *Phoenix Daniels*

Natasha smiled and grabbed Bella's hand. "Thank you," she whispered. "I took an overnighter from Paris for this."

Bella squeezed Natasha's hand in return and smile. "Alright then. Let's go and burn this motherfuckah to the ground," Bella asserted.

"Let's do it!" Victoria hailed.

Bella pulled the radio from her back pocket. She pressed the call button. "Hit it!"

Bella turned around and stood next to Victoria and Natasha. Together, they watched SWAT, one of the world's best high-risk entry teams, breach the abandoned book factory located on the west side of Chicago.

After months of listening to audio tapes, produced by a paranoid sociopath, and meticulously tracking down every single lead, Bella was finally ready to annihilate the massive human trafficking operation.

Nothing could compare to the sound of the battering ram hitting the door and shattering a realm of fear, pain, human suffering, and oppression. She listened to the chatter on the radio until SWAT declared that the building had been cleared.

"Let's go," Bella said to Victoria and Natasha.

CREED 2
by *Phoenix Daniels*

The three of them jogged across the street and entered the factory. At first sight, there was nothing to see. But as they advanced further into the building, they were smack dab in the middle of what looked like barracks. There were several 15x10 rooms that housed at least ten sets of bunk beds, and even some baby beds. Scared and half-naked women and children were huddled together in the corners of each of the rooms.

SWAT stood to the side as the VICE unit led handcuffed offenders out of the front door. Once the building was free from offenders, Social Services, along with other government agencies entered. They began to render aid to victimized women and children.

Bella stopped an EMT as he escorted one of the women out of the building. She gave the woman a reassuring smile as she reached for her hand. The woman was fully compliant when Bella turned her hand to examine her wrist. As expected, she had the same type of barcode tattooed on her flesh like the three dead girls in the abandoned house.

Bella looked over at the Storm women. Neither was trying to hide their despair. Natasha swiped a tear from her cheek as Victoria pulled her into her arms. Bella never really knew what had happened to Natasha when she was abducted by human traffickers, but looking at her, it wasn't hard to deduce that it had been a horrific experience. Both, Natasha and Victoria had survived horrific experiences.

Bella slowly approached them and placed her arms around them

"It is done," she whispered, hoping that the results of the raid would provide them with some comfort.

EPILOGUE

TAYLOR

Taylor stood on the balcony and marveled at the beauty of the gardens of the executive mansion. Admittedly, Taylor had had reservations about getting married at the governor's mansion. She didn't want a stuffy, pretentious wedding. It was bad enough that a slew of politicians was going be in attendance. But the grounds of the executive mansion were nothing short of breathtaking and not to mention convenient.

She and Victor had gone through so much. Between making the arrangements for Rosemary's funeral, battling the press, and planning their wedding, Taylor just wanted easy.

"Taylor, baby, if you plan on gettin' married, you better get in this dress," Taylor's mom, Martha, called out from the dressing room.

Taylor's satin robe danced in the warm, May breeze as she walked through the Victorian-inspired doors. As soon as she entered the dressing room, she saw Nicole and her mom holding her wedding dress with tears swimming in their eyes. Bella narrowed her eyes and crossed her arms.

CREED 2
by *Phoenix Daniels*

"If that woman comes in here and shoves me in that chair again because y'all made me cry, I am gonna be *sooo* mad."

The smile on her mom's face warmed Taylor's heart. Over the years, Martha Montgomery has made no secret of her desire for Taylor and Nicole to get married and produce grandchildren. They all assumed that Nicole would be the first to jump the broom, but Victor came along and shook things up.

"Wait!" Victoria called out.

She and Bella came hurrying across the room. Victoria was carrying two bottles of Veuve Clicquot, and Bella was carrying champagne flutes. Both were beautiful in their bride's maid's dresses. Taylor had allowed all of her attendants to choose their own design and color, as long as it was cohesive with her modern monarchy themed wedding. Victoria chose royal blue, and Bella chose burgundy.

"We need to knock back a couple before you step into that gorgeous gown," Bella suggested, handing Taylor a glass.

Victoria carefully poured champagne into Taylor's glass. She turned to Martha and Nicole. "You too. Put that dress down and have a little sippy sip."

CREED 2
by *Phoenix Daniels*

Martha chuckled and shook her head at Bella and Victoria. "The two of you are a bad influence. But I guess we have time for a toast."

Martha and Nicole carefully placed the gown on a chaise lounger, spreading the long train so that it wouldn't wrinkle.

"Now we drink," Bella declared.

Taylor watched as Bella handed out glasses, and Victoria poured. Seeing the two of them working together was something that she thought she'd never see. Victoria and Bella, settling their differences had allowed Taylor to be closer to them both. She was definitely happier not being the friend in the middle of a beef between friends.

"Wait for me!" Maria shouted as she exited the bathroom.

She was stunning in her bronze, Victorian off-the-shoulder bride's maid gown. Bella handed her a glass, and Victoria filled it. Taylor looked around the room, proud of the strong, beautiful women that she'd been blessed enough to have in her life.

Taylor cleared her throat to silence the chatter and get the ladies attention. Once the room was silent, Taylor raised her glass.

CREED 2
by *Phoenix Daniels*

"Since my enablers insisted that I get boozed up before I say I do, I feel the need to propose a toast. It has not been an easy road traveled to get to this point, but it was definitely worth it. I want you all to know that I wouldn't be here if it wasn't for the love and support of the dynamic, strong, loyal, fierce, and the beautiful women surrounding me. I love each and every last one of you."

Taylor could feel the moisture pooling in her eyes. Earlier, at Nicole's insistence, she'd sat in a makeup chair for over an hour. Since she had no intention of returning to that chair, Taylor raised her glass higher and concluded her toast.

"To you!" she shouted

Taylor and the ladies took a sip from their glasses.

"Hey, y'all," Taylor called out before the chatter could resume. "I need y'all to hurry up and knock that shit so that I can go and marry the man of my dreams."

The ladies laughed and did as instructed. Soon, they were all scrambling around the room, getting ready for Taylor's big day.

BELLA

After the most exquisite wedding that that Bella had ever witnessed, she stood in the elaborate ballroom of the executive mansion, sipping champagne. The place was filled with the world's elite and high-ranking political officials. Bella was most definitely socializing above her station.

"Taylor looks amazing," Donatella whispered.

Bella nodded in agreement. Taylor was a vision of loveliness in a vintage, white, tulle and lace, off-the-shoulder wedding gown. Her thick, natural hair was pulled into a high bun, encircled in a diamond crown with a beautiful lace veil attached to the back. The gorgeous backdrop of the garden was no comparison to the exquisite bride.

"You and Lucas have been joined at the hip for a while now. You 'bout ready to jump the broom, baby sis?" Donatella asked before lifting her glass to her mouth.

"Neither one of us is in a big hurry to get married. We're having too much fun shacking up."

"I heard that," Donatella mumbled.

CREED 2
by *Phoenix Daniels*

Bella looked around the fancy ballroom for Lucas. When she spotted him, he was huddled in the corner with his brothers.

"Girl, that is one perfect gene pool. A bitch could just go, eeny meeny miny moe, and come out a winner."

"Naw, bitch," Bella scoffed. "You can go, eeny meeny or miny, because moe and *mine* are taken."

Donatella laughed. "Don't nobody want your man."

"Yeah, I figured. Since you can't seem to take your eyes off Linc. I know you fucked him," Bella muttered.

"Oh, and, how do you know that?" Donna retorted, rolling her eyes. "You got a twin sense that I don't have? I definitely don't remember feeling you cum when Lucas was rodding your ass out."

"Mm-hm. You fucked him." Bella snickered.

"Whatever," Donatella dismissed.

"Yeah, whatever, Telly."

She giggled and walked away from her sister. She was missing Lucas, but she'd only made it halfway to him when the wedding coordinator announced the throwing of the bouquet. Bella kept walking, ignoring the announcement. But she was cut short when Tabitha Creed blocked her path. The serious look on her face concerned Bella.

"What's the matter?"

Lucas' mother narrowed her eyes at Bella. She had absolutely no idea what she could have done to piss Dr. Creed off.

"What? What's wrong?" Bella asked.

"Get your narrow behind over there and catch that damn bouquet, Belladonna Devereaux," Tabitha gritted.

Bella sighed, relieved that she hadn't pissed of the matriarch of the Creed family. She began to laugh, but when she noticed that Tabitha wasn't laughing with her, she stopped. Bella held her hands up in surrender. She looked past Lucas' mom to see her man and his brothers laughing at her. Bella took two steps back, turned on her heel, and acquiesced.

"I-I'm just gonna go over there and catch that bouquet," Bella muttered.

She reluctantly walked over to the group of giddy, single women, hoping to snag a husband, and waited for Taylor to toss the bouquet.

After a short countdown, Bella was nearly smacked in the face by the bundle of flowers. She looked up at Taylor and frowned. Taylor's agenda was obvious to everyone in the ballroom. Bella wondered if she and Tabitha, together, had cooked up the scheme to feed Bella the bouquet.

Taylor smirked and began a round of applause to celebrate Bella's so-called victory. Playing along, Bella raised the bouquet over her head and took a bow.

"I guess that means that you're next, huh?" Lucas teased from behind.

Bella turned around and snaked her arms around his neck. She inhaled the scent that she longed for when he wasn't near.

"I guess so," she whispered.

Lucas wrapped an arm around her waist and pulled her closer. "Got anyone in mind?"

"Not yet," Bella teased. "But I'll let you know when I find someone."

Lucas narrowed his eyes and smack Bella's behind. "Don't play with me, girl. You know I'm gonna make you my wife."

Bella looked into her man's beautiful jade eyes, and for the first time, she was able to imagine herself getting married again. Bella rose on her toes and kissed his warm, soft lips.

CREED 2
by Phoenix Daniels

With his hand pressed into the small of her back, Lucas deepened the kiss. Bella savored the taste of mint and passion as their shared affection united them. Remembering that they weren't alone, Bella lowered herself, momentarily severing their connection.

"Lucas, you couldn't possibly understand how much I love you."

"Belladonna, if it's half as much as I love you, we'll be indestructible."

THE END